Chronicles

of the

Initiations

Additional Books by
Jason Edwards:

Will Allen and the Great Monster Detective
Chronicles of the Monster Detective Agency – Volume 1
(chapter book version)

Will Allen and the Ring of Terror
Chronicles of the Monster Detective Agency – Volume 2
(chapter book version)

Will Allen and the Hideous Shroud
Chronicles of the Monster Detective Agency – Volume 3

Will Allen and the Terrible Truth
Chronicles of the Monster Detective Agency – Volume 4

Chronicles
of the
Monster Detective Agency

Initiations

Jason Edwards

Rogue Bear Press
New York

For information regarding permission, write to:

Rogue Bear Press, PO Box #513, Ardsley, NY 10502

ISBN 13 : 9780978951276

Library of Congress Catalog # 2014951504

Text copyright © 2007, 2015 by Jeffrey Friedman

Illustrations copyright © 2007, 2009, 2015 by Jeffrey Friedman

All rights reserved. Published by Rogue Bear Press.
Home of great books and engaging interACTIVE enrichment programs for schools and libraries including :

 and

 Check the programs' websites for
more information, or visit us at
ROGUEBEARPRESS.COM

First Printing - July 2015 Printed in the U.S.A.

READING LEVEL RATINGS :

This book is rated level III in the Rogue Bear Press *Accele*Reader Program.

It is designed for children 8-15 years of age.

Metametrics Lexile Reading Level : 670L

Learn more about our *Accele*Reader Program at RogueBearPress.com.

To **Jenna** *and* **Jessica,**
who I hope will learn, as I did
that inspiration can spring to life
from the strangest of places

Contents

Chapter One – The Problem Solvers

You know, when you're being hung upside down from your ankle like a side of beef while vicious fangs are snapping at you from every direction, there is only room for one thought in your panic-stricken brain.

"How do I get myself into these things?" I grumbled as a pair of drooling, fanged jaws came flying right at my face.

Now I know that may seem like a bit of an unusual situation to find yourself in, but you see, my name is Will Allen, and I'm a monster detective.

Yes, you read that right: I'm a monster detective. And no, I'm not talking about some fantasy role-playing game. I fight monsters. The big, slobbery kind that would like nothing better than to use your head as a chew toy.

Mind you, you'd never guess that I'm a monster detective if you met me since I'm not one of those... well, *detective*-looking kinds of guys. You know the ones I mean, don't you? Big as apes, tough as nails, with faces that look like they were chiseled out of granite? Well I'm nothing like that: in fact, I'm one of the shortest and skinniest kids in my whole school. And I don't know what things are like where *you* live, but at Ashford Middle School being scrawny and smart is not a ticket to being adored by your classmates, I can tell you that. Still, a little person can solve some really big challenges, and in my time as a detective I've cracked some of the biggest, strangest cases you could ever imagine. But not one of them was any stranger than how I got started doing this in the first place.

I wasn't always a detective, you see. I mean I've always had a knack for solving mysteries - in fact, when I was a little kid my dad said that if figuring out whodunits was a game show, I'd make him a fortune. I often showed my detective-like skills at home, which is why sometimes my mom would say something like, "That's amazing Will! How did you know I baked cookies while you were out? I cleaned everything up and even aired out the kitchen so you wouldn't smell them!" and I would tell her, "Easy, mom. There's a trace of flour on the counter, the oven door is warm, and you hid something in the breadbox real fast when I came in."

And every now and then my dad would say something like, "Will, how in the world did you find my golf club? I've been looking for it for days!" and I would answer, "Simple, dad. I knew that the last time you practiced in the yard, you trimmed the shrubs after, so I looked behind the rack where the pruning shears go."

Yeah, I've always been a whiz when it comes to solving mysteries, especially the really tricky ones that other people can't seem to crack.

Well, most of the time, anyway. Sometimes even I needed help, which is where my story begins. You see, I had this problem. But it wasn't a lost toy, or too much gel squirting out of the toothpaste tube, or any of those stupid little problems that some other kids have.

I had a monster under my bed.

Now, if you're like everybody else, you're probably thinking: *A monster? Oh, come on! There's no such thing.*

To be honest, I'd probably react the same way if I hadn't had one myself. After all, who wouldn't? So naturally, no one believed me.

Certainly not my parents.

"I have a monster under my bed," I said to my dad one morning as he sat at the table hiding behind his daily newspaper. He glared at me over the top of the business section.

"Don't be ridiculous. We don't believe in monsters," he replied, then ruffled the paper and turned to the next page. That didn't exactly make me feel better, so I went to my mom, who was in the kitchen putting our breakfast plates into the dishwasher.

"I have a monster under my bed," I told her.

"Well, don't invite it to tea," she answered without looking up. "We're down to four cups already, and some invisible monster always seems to break things around here."

In case you were wondering, that was my mother trying to be funny. She's not very good at it.

I decided not to tell anyone at school about the monster, because most kids will give you a weird look or something if you tell them stuff like that. But I *did* tell my friend, Jeannine. She likes solving mysteries almost as much as I do, and we've always helped each other figure out the especially tricky ones, so I knew I could count on her.

"I have a monster under my bed," I whispered quietly as we sat together on the bus to school. She gave me a weird look. Go figure.

Of course, a weird look from Jeannine is a little different from other people's weird looks, mostly because Jeannine looks a little weird to begin with, seeing as how she likes to wear lots of bright, tie-dyed clothes, color her hair with streaks of purple, green, and blue, and hang paperclips from her ears.

"Oh, Will," she said. "It's not fair! You always have the coolest things happen to you."

Now I gave *her* a weird look.

4

"What could possibly be cool about having a monster under my bed?" I asked.

"Well, it's way cooler than the plain old dust bunnies I have under mine," she answered.

Personally, I didn't think a monster under my bed was cool at all, but Jeannine sometimes has sort of a *different* way of looking at things.

"At least dust bunnies don't try to lure you under the bed so they can eat you," I pointed out.

Jeannine's head twitched, and then she nodded as she thought that over.

"Well, okay, there's *that*," she finally said. "But still, it's way interesting."

"It is not!" I growled. "We're 6th graders now, Jeannine! 6th graders don't have monsters! It is definitely not cool!"

"It *could* be," Jeannine insisted. "It depends on what kind of monster it is. What does yours look like?"

"I don't know," I said. "I've never actually gotten a good look at it. It only comes out when it's really dark."

"You've never seen it?" Her face went sour, like it does when she sees that her mom has given her a bag of snow peas for her snack again. "Then how do you even know you have a monster?"

"Well for one thing, it makes noises," I told her. "Like…weird scratching and gurgling sounds."

"Maybe it's a chipmunk," she said.

My cheeks started to burn. Believe me, you don't want to be around when they get really fired up.

"Don't you think I thought of that?" I growled. "When I check during the day, nothing is there. No scratch marks. No nutshells. And I looked over every inch of the walls and ceiling. There are no holes or cracks that it could come in through."

"Maybe it's a mouse crawling under the floorboards."

"The sounds I hear aren't coming from under the floorboards!" I hissed. "And mice don't grab your quilt and pull it under your bed while you sleep so that you'll get cold and come down after it. Only monsters do that!"

Jeannine gave me a blank stare, and then began fiddling with one of the gothic skull rings on her fingers.

"Well then," she finally said. "I guess you have a monster under your bed."

"Exactly," I agreed.

"So, what are you going to do about it?" She replied without missing a beat.

"I'm not sure," I said. "I tried to set a trap for it, but I couldn't lure it out into the open."

"What did you use as bait?" she asked.

"A brownie ice cream sundae," I told her. "I figured that would attract almost anything."

Jeannine looked quite shocked.

"And it *didn't work*?" she gasped.

"Nope," I replied. "Plus my parents yelled at me when the ice cream melted all over the floor."

Jeannine scratched her head, which is what she does when she tries to think too hard. Only this time, she came up with a really good idea.

"What we need," she said, "is to find an expert: someone who has experience dealing with stuff like this and can tell you what to do."

My eyes grew wide and I gaped at her with a *why didn't I think of that* look on my face.

"That's a very good idea," I said. Jeannine smiled.

"Thank you," she said.

"Um...where do you suppose we could find someone like that?" I asked.

Jeannine stopped smiling, and started scratching her head again. Just then, the bus pulled into the school parking lot.

"Well, I'm sure we'll think of something," she said. And then without another word, she got up and walked off the bus. Some people get annoyed when she does stuff like that, but to me that's just Jeannine being Jeannine. A few seconds later, I followed.

Chapter Two – Secondary Troubles

In the two months since we had started there, Jeannine and I decided that Ashford Middle School was a pretty decent place, but I had a rather bad day there that day, owing to my getting caught by Mrs. McAllister leafing through the yellow pages when I was supposed to be doing math problems.

"And *what* do you think you are doing?" she said as she walked over and stood above me.

"Um, I'd rather not say," I told her.

For some reason, Mrs. McAllister got very stern. Her painted-on black eyebrows, which clashed sharply with her silver-grey hair, rose high above her thick, horn-rimmed glasses.

"You will explain yourself this instant, or go straight to the principal's office!" she roared.

I looked down and bit my lip.

"Well?" she said impatiently.

"I'm thinking it over," I said.

Mrs. McAllister's pale cheeks turned red. She grabbed the book.

"The yellow pages?" The expression on her face changed from angry to puzzled. "Why are you looking for...an exterminator?"

"I...ah, have a *pest* problem at home."

"I see," she growled. "And you are looking for an exterminator...in *my* math class? Why aren't your parents taking care of this?"

"They don't take math," I said.

I got a lot of extra homework to do that day.

When I got on the bus to go home, Jeannine had already saved me a seat, just as she has ever since second grade.

"So, I solved your problem!" she gushed.

"You did?" I sputtered. "How?"

"I figured out where to find you an expert!" she said, patting herself on the back proudly.

"Really?" I said, perking up brightly. "Where?"

"Just check the yellow pages!" she answered. "Look under 'E' for exterminators."

My grateful smile melted into a nasty scowl. I turned away and made a loud *Harrumpf* sound.

"What?" she said. "What did I say?"

"Never mind," I grumbled. "I already looked."

"You didn't find any ads for exterminators?"

"Not the kind I need."

"Then what's that?" she said, pointing at my book bag.

"What's what?" I asked.

"That card sticking out of your bag," she answered. She tilted her head slantways, and read, "M-O-N-S-T-..." Her head popped upright again. "That's all I can see, but I'm pretty sure it says something about monsters."

I pulled my bag off my back and looked at the pocket. Sure enough, there was a card sticking out. I plucked it out of my bag and read it out loud.

11

Monster Detective Agency

Bigelow Hawkins
Detective First Class

specializing in identification and eradication of all types of ghouls and beasties

No Fee

"Look," I said. "There's a handwritten note on the back of the card."

"What does it say?" Jeannine asked.

"It says, 'If you need me, hang a red flag out your window.'"

"Well," Jeannine said. "It looks like you found your expert monster hunter."

I shook my head. "I didn't. It looks like *he* found *me*."

"Whatever," she said with a wave of her hand. "The point is: your problem is solved."

But I wasn't so sure. I've been the butt of enough pranks to be suspicious of mysterious messages telling me to do things.

"But how did he find me? How did he know I was looking for a... I mean, I didn't tell anyone but you about..." I stopped and held my breath for a second, then looked all around the bus to be sure no one was listening. There were a couple of cheerleaders and a big brute in a football team jacket filling the seats right behind us, so I ducked my head and whispered, "...About my *you know what*."

"Maybe someone heard us this morning," Jeannine answered. "Maybe word got around to someone who's been through this too."

"So then you think someone on the bus knew where to find a monster detective, and put the card in my bag?" I said skeptically. "I doubt it. It's probably just somebody playing a prank, like that time when those guys from the football team tricked Mico Markowitz into hanging his shorts from the flagpole."

Jeannine rolled her eyes at me, and said, "Well, so what if it is? All it's asking you to do is hang a flag out your window. Just do it and see what happens."

"But I don't have a red flag."

"A red shirt then," Jeannine insisted. "What's the difference?"

"Nope. I don't have one of those either."

Jeannine frowned, and then started scratching her head again.

"Do you have a red flag I could borrow?" I asked her.

"No," she said. "My parents think red flags are un-American."

"A red shirt?"

"No. My mother says red is not my color."

"Do you have *anything* red?"

"Well, if you're desperate, I have some old red panties in the back of my drawer. I wouldn't mind you hanging *them* out a window."

Hang girl's panties out my window? I thought. *Seriously?*

"I'd rather be eaten by the monster," I muttered.

Jeannine got a little snippy after that.

"Suit yourself," she said, tilting her nose up and turning away.

Girls can be so moody sometimes. I tried to talk to her some more after that, but she just told me that I'd have to figure something out on my own.

When I got home, I went to my room and started my homework, but I didn't get much done. I sat at my desk beneath my Chicago Cubs pennant and my poster of Albert Einstein, the only things hanging on the annoyingly cheerful blue wallpaper, and was busy coloring in the 'O's on my second sheet of math problems when an idea hit me. I hunted down my dad's special Fourth of July American Flag and rolled it up halfway, so that only the red and white stripes showed. Then I started coloring in the white stripes with red magic marker. That's when my mom came in. Her dirty blonde curls were wrapped in a hairnet and her smock was covered in fresh splatters of paint, so I knew she'd just come from her studio in the basement.

"Are you doing homework?" she asked.

"Um, sort of..." I answered.

Oops. Never say 'sort of' to a mom. It makes her think you're up to something. My mom came over for a closer look, and when she saw what I was doing, her eyes popped out.

No, I don't mean *out of her head and rolling on the floor* out, she just got all bug-eyed.

"Will!" she cried out in horror. "What have you done?"

The shrill tone in her voice made me shudder. When I glanced up, I saw the same scowl pasted on her face that she wore the day she found me building an igloo in the living room.

"Ummmm... Is that a trick question?" I asked.

"The flag!" she shouted. "Our American flag!   You've ruined it!"

I looked back down at the flag. Three stripes were colored in, and one was halfway finished.

"They're washable markers, mom."

"Give me that this instant!"

"But mom, I *need* it..."

"This instant!" she shouted. Her cheeks were as red as the flag, so I knew there was no point in arguing. I handed her the flag.

"I'm going to speak to your father about this!" she said in that *'You're in SUCH big trouble'* kind of voice that she has. "Desecrating the flag! Do you know you could go to jail for that?"

"Do the beds there have monsters under them?" I asked.

My mom stormed out without speaking another word. Personally, I don't see what the big deal was all about, but there's something about flags that makes grownups act weird. But now, I was back to square one, with no flag, and no monster hunter.

"I'd better put on my thinking cap," I said to myself.

And no, I am not too old for a thinking cap.

Anyway, I don't actually have a cap, but just saying that somehow makes me think better. And sure enough, I came up with another idea. But I figured I'd better wait until after dinner to test out my new plan so that my mom wouldn't catch me again. So, after sitting down at the table that evening to a meal with a French name that my mom took twenty minutes trying to get me to pronounce, but which *I* called, "old socks with brown sauce," I went back up to my room and got out a white t-shirt from my underwear drawer. I tied the sleeves together around the end of my baseball bat, and when I hung it sideways, it *sort of* looked like a flag.

"Now I just have to make it red," I told myself. But I had already used up all the ink in my red makers, so I went to the kitchen and got some fruit punch from the refrigerator. I took the bottle back to my room and poured the drink all over the white shirt. When it was pretty much soaked, I stopped and held it up. It was kind of blotchy and purplish, but hey, I figured maybe it's close enough. I took my bat and jammed it into my clothes hamper, and then moved it to the window and hung the shirt through the opening. Then I closed the window as much as I could and hoped for the best.

All of a sudden, a creepy voice came from right behind me.

Chapter Three – A Most Unusual Detective

"I knew you'd call," spoke a low, squeaky, yet gravelly kind of voice. I turned around really fast, and there, standing next to my bed, was a very, very small person in a very, very big trench coat and bowler hat. Aside from a shiny gold badge on the ratty old coat, I couldn't make out much: the coat covered everything right down to the ground, including his hands and feet, and a dark, fuzzy nose and a mess of scraggly brown hair were all that poked out from under the brim of the hat.

"Are you the monster hunter?" I asked.

"Detective," the gravelly voice replied, pointing proudly at his badge. "Monster *Detective*, Bigelow J. Hawkins at your service."

He looked more like a munchkin in disguise.

"Aren't you a little short for a detective?"

"Size isn't everything," Bigelow answered. "A little person can solve some really big cases. I myself have uncovered some of the biggest monsters there are."

"And you can get rid of them?"

Bigelow gave me a strange look. At least I think he did, because his face barely showed from under his hat, but he slouched as though he was sad.

"I usually don't have to. Once we find your monster, all we have to do is shine some light on it. Monsters hate light."

"That makes them disappear?"

He sighed, and then shook his head.

"No. That makes them...less scary. And monsters that aren't scary don't have much reason to hang around."

"Oh," I said. "Well, that sounds good enough for me. Let's get started."

"We can't. Not yet," Bigelow said.

"What? Why not?"

"It's not dark yet. I told you, monsters don't like the light. They won't come out until nighttime. That's when we'll uncover them."

He then walked over to the light switch on my wall and turned it off. The room darkened somewhat, but some faint, fiery rays from the setting sun continued to filter in through my window, making the walls glow eerily. The air turned stale and cold.

"Um, what should we do until then?" I asked.

"Well, for a start, let's discuss my fee," Bigelow answered. My face went sour.

"Your *fee?*" I said rather crossly. "Your card said there wasn't any fee."

"You must have read it wrong," Bigelow insisted. "Look again. It says 'No fee *unless successful*'."

I took out the card, which I'd kept in my pocket since the bus ride from school, and read it over.

Monster Detective Agency

Bigelow Hawkins
Detective First Class

Specializing in identification and eradication of all types of ghouls and beasties

No Fee unless successful

"Huh. How about that?" I said. "Well, how much do you want? I've been saving up for a new bicycle, but..."

"Oh, I don't accept cash," Bigelow said. "But I believe you have an old teddy bear that you don't play with anymore. I'd like that."

"My Teddy? You want to be paid with a *toy*?" I said. "Are you serious?"

I tried to get a better look at him, and leaned forward so that I could see beneath the brim of his hat, but it was too dark under there to see his face.

"That's my price," he answered firmly, "for helping you solve your monster problem. Do you want my help or not?"

Like it or not, I needed help. I went to my toy chest and dug down to the bottom until I uncovered Teddy. He was a little ratty, but still soft and warm.

"But...I don't want to give him up." I pouted.

"You don't play with him anymore."

"I know. But he's still...*special* to me."

"I promise," he said in a voice that sounded much less gravelly, "that I will take good care of him, and give him a home where he'll always be happy."

I looked down at Teddy. I swear it almost looked like he smiled.

"Well, okay," I finally said, and handed him to Bigelow. At that very moment, the room turned dark. The cheerful blue color fled from my walls, turning them to shades of mud.

"What...what's happening?" I asked, looking around nervously.

"They're coming," Bigelow whispered. "Night is falling."

"But how did it get dark so fast?"

"Never mind," he grumbled. "Let's just get ready. Where's your RevealeR?"

"My what?"

"Your RevealeR," Bigelow said. "You know, a flashlight that can shine some light on the monsters."

"I...I don't have one," I whispered nervously. Right then, it got *much* darker. The air around us grew thick with an inky mist, and the shadows from the trickle of light that dripped in through the window crawled all around us. But Bigelow ignored all that.

"Here, have this one," Bigelow whispered back, handing me a worn, weathered-looking red flashlight from behind his back. The casing tingled, and when it touched my fingers a burst of heat shot through me.

"Whoa! I hope this thing isn't broken," I muttered, and then flicked the switch with my thumb. A soft hum arose and light poured out, but it was a very strange light: it was a little greenish, and sort of fizzy, like a stream of soap bubbles.

"Don't turn it on yet!" he hissed. "You'll scare him off!" I turned the flashlight off quickly.

"Sorry," I said quietly. "What do we do now?"

"We wait," he answered.

So we sat there in the dark, as quiet as mice, for the better part of an hour. Finally, Bigelow got up, turned on his flashlight, and paced around the room.

"This isn't working," he muttered.

"Does that mean I get Teddy back?"

Bigelow turned to face me. There in the dark, he seemed much bigger than he had earlier.

"What we need," he declared, "is to set a trap."

"I already tried that," I told him.

"What did you use as bait?"

"A brownie ice-cream sundae."

Bigelow seemed shocked.

"And it *didn't work*?" he gasped.

"No," I said.

Bigelow scratched his head, doing the same thinking scratch that Jeannine did all the time.

"I have an idea," he finally announced.

"Really? What?"

"We need different bait," he said. "I think I know what will lure him out into the open."

"What do we need?"

Instead of answering, Bigelow looked me over. As he turned his head up, I thought for a second that I saw his eyes glow from under that bowler hat.

"Go sit in the middle of the room," he ordered. I instantly obeyed. My parents would have died of shock if they knew.

"Good," he said. "Now, whatever you hear, just stay where you are."

"Whatever you hear? What does *that* mean?"

But Bigelow just said, "Hush now," so I sat there, alone, in the middle of the room. I know it sounds crazy, but I could swear the walls were creeping closer, and as the shadows grew deeper, I shuddered from a sudden chill.

"N...Now what?" I stuttered.

"Now just listen," he whispered.

I listened, but the darkness seemed to be sucking all the sound right out of the air. Just when it seemed as if nothing could break through, I heard a swooshing and rustling sound.

"Is that it?" I asked. "Is that the monster?"

Bigelow then did a strange thing. Even though it was very dark, he pulled out a magnifying glass, put it to his eye, and scanned the room. The glass itself had a faint, greenish aura, but if Bigelow was seeing anything creepy through it, he didn't say.

"No," he finally answered. "That's just the wind blowing through the trees."

I listened harder. Deep in the mist, there was a creepy, creaking sound.

"That's it, isn't it?" I whispered fiercely. Bigelow scanned again.

"No," he said. "Just loose floorboards."

The whooshing and creaking died away, and it grew very quiet. There in the stillness, the shadows became like living things, closing in on me like hungry wolves. That's when I heard something else, something that made my skin tingle and goose-bumps pop up all over.

It was a scratching sound coming from under the bed. Then there was a gurgling, and I looked all around to see what it was. But all I saw was darkness.

"B...Bigelow? Is that you?"

But Bigelow didn't answer. All I heard was the gurgling sound, which grew into a growl, like that of an empty stomach. It seemed to be moving all around me.

And it was getting closer.

Chapter Four – Nightfall

The situation was bad. I sensed that I was in terrible danger.

Danger of dumping a load into my undershorts, that is. One more second and I would have needed some toilet tissue, a mop, and a new pair of pants, but just then my door opened and light poured into the room. My father walked in and said, "Will! Why are you sitting in the dark? Don't you know it's bad for your eyes?" And he turned on the light.

"There, that's better," he said, and then looked around the room. "What were you doing in here?"

I blinked from the sudden brightness, and then looked around. The noises had vanished, and the tingling in my skin disappeared. Bigelow was nowhere to be seen, but as I scanned the room searching for him, I noticed that my teddy bear now sat on my bed next to the pillow. When I bent down to look under the bed, my father stopped me.

"Are you hiding something under there?"

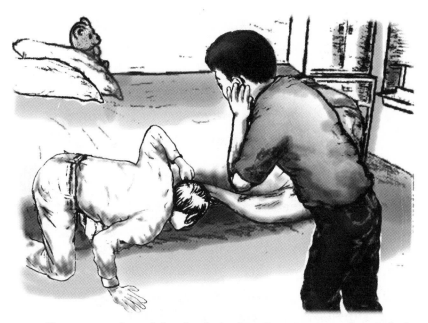

He stooped and looked under, but I guess he didn't see anything, because he stood right back up and looked around. That's when he noticed Teddy.

"What's *that* doing here?" He reached to pick Teddy up, but I rushed over and grabbed him first. When I squeezed him close, away from my father's grasp, I could swear I felt him grow warm all over.

"Oh, for Pete's sake," my dad said irritably. "Aren't you getting a little old for a teddy bear?"

I didn't say anything. I just clung tighter to Teddy. I don't know if it was Teddy or me, but one of us felt like pouring a load of hot sauce into my dad's evening tea.

I don't think it was Teddy.

"What do you want, dad?" I grumbled in a surly tone. "Are you looking to borrow another comic book?"

My dad blushed. Now, I knew my mother must have sent him to scold me about the flag, but I could tell by the way he was scrunching his eyebrows that he had forgotten why he had come, and I certainly wasn't going to help him remember.

"Never mind," my father finally said. "Just get ready for bed. And get rid of that...that horrible thing."

I froze. Had he spotted Bigelow? Or the monster?

"What thing?" I said, looking all around. "Where?"

"I meant the bear," he said, and left, closing the door behind him. Right away, I began searching the room for Bigelow. As I rifled through my closet to see if he was hiding there, I heard it again: the scratching noise under my bed. I slowly walked on over, then bent down and thrust the flashlight ahead of me as I looked underneath.

There was Bigelow, his magnifying glass held close to his eye, bent over inspecting the floorboards.

"Bigelow!" I shouted. "There you are!"

Bigelow looked up at me, and through the magnifying glass his eye looked like a huge, hairy crystal ball.

"Well of course I'm here," he said irritably. "Where else would you search for a monster that's under your bed?"

"But there's nothing there," I said. "My dad just looked."

It was hard to be sure, but Bigelow shook his head like he was rolling his eyes at me.

"Grownups," he grumbled. "Don't know monsters from meatballs."

"Well, that explains last night's dinner," I said.

"Never trust a grownup to find a monster," Bigelow insisted. "I've never yet met one who can."

"What are you saying?" I asked. "That grownups can't see monsters?"

"Just the opposite," he answered gruffly. "They see them *everywhere*. But their monsters look a lot different than yours. They look like a neighbor who might be a kidnapper, or the new manager who might steal their job, or the new building that's going to cut off their scenic views and lower their property values. And so they just can't imagine how monsters could look anything like what yours do."

I thought about all that for a minute.

"What...what do *my* monsters look like?" I finally asked.

Bigelow pursed his lips, and tapped them with the end of his flashlight.

"We'll see," he said, and then he walked over to the light switch and turned it off once more. The room went nearly pitch black, and I trembled as the shadows sprang back to life. My head twitched back and forth, scanning the room for any sign of movement, when suddenly the scratching sound came back. It echoed off every wall, and I turned on my flashlight and pointed it all around.

"Not yet!" Bigelow shouted. "Turn it off!"

"But...but how can I find the monster if I can't see him?"

"Don't worry," Bigelow assured. "He'll find *you*."

He'll find YOU? I didn't like the sound of that *AT ALL*.

"But I don't want him to find me!" I cried. "I just want him to go away!"

"Will," he said in as calm and steady a tone as his squeaky, gravelly voice could manage, "this is the only way. If you don't face your monster, you'll never be rid of him. Never."

My shaking hands turned and shined the light right at Bigelow, using the very flashlight he had put in my grasp. Bigelow squinted as the strange, greenish light washed over him, but he didn't flinch.

"Be brave, Will," he said. "You can do it."

Someone more sensible than me would probably have thought twice before turning off the light in a room with a lurking monster, which to me seemed kind of like lighting a match in a dynamite factory, but for some reason I trusted Bigelow. I turned off my flashlight, and waves of darkness poured in to fill the space where the beam had been.

"Good," he said, as the scratching noise grew into a growl again. "Now, what do you hear?"

"A monster." I answered. "And he sounds hungry."

"Is he...*saying* anything?"

"What would he say?" I asked tersely. "Lunchtime?"

Even over the growling, I could hear the sound of Bigelow scratching his head.

"All right," he grumbled. "Let's try something. Act like you're really scared."

"Try to act scared?" I snarled. "Really? *That's* your brilliant idea? I'd rather try staying off tonight's menu!"

"Actually, monsters don't have menus. They..."

"Never mind! I've had enough of this already! I'm turning the light back on."

But when I flicked the switch on my flashlight, it sputtered and shook, but nothing came out. The room actually grew darker, and shadows began swirling across the floor. My knees started shaking.

"Uh, Bigelow...the flashlight..."

My breath became frosty, and the growling sound grew much louder, so loud that it became a roar.

"Yes, that's it!" Bigelow urged. "Now, what do you hear?"

"A...a roaring," I said through chattering teeth. "Wait, it sounds like..."

Rising above the roaring was another gurgling, and then a sloshing sound.

"It sounds like..."

A glub-glubbing sound replaced the sloshing. That was when it hit me.

"It sounds like...a *toilet flushing!*"

"Now!" Bigelow shouted. "Turn on your RevealeR and shine the light on it now!"

"But mine doesn't work!"

"Oh, nonsense!" Bigelow insisted. "Try again!"

I flicked the switch once more, and this time there was a powerful hum, and the beam came right on.

Then I kind of wished it was still broken.

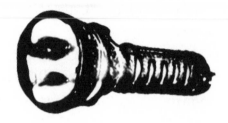

Chapter Five – What Lurks in the Darkness

I swung the beam of light up and down and it revealed, bit by bit, the form of what stood before me. At first there was just a shiny gleam from the smooth white surface. Then I saw a reflection from a bright brass handle, and foaming water splashing out the sides.

"It...it can't be..." I whispered.

But as impossible as it might seem, there in the middle of my room was a giant *toilet*, stretching from the floor almost to the ceiling, with big bulging eyes on top and rows of sharp, shark-like teeth sticking out from between the seat and the bowl.

"B...Bigelow?" I called out weakly.

"I'm here, Will," he answered.

"Bigelow?" I repeated. "I...I have to pee!"

"Not now!" he shouted. "Fight it!"

"I am fighting it!" I protested. "But I really have to go! I drank a whole chocolate-tofu milkshake for dessert! And that stuff just runs right through me!"

"I meant the *monster*," Bigelow growled. "Fight it! Use the light!"

I couldn't believe what I was hearing.

"You want me to fight a ten foot tall man-eating toilet...with a *flashlight*?"

"With your *bravery*!" he urged. "You can do it, Will! I know you have it in you!"

Personally, I was thinking less about having it in me, and more about that toilet having *me* in *it*. And believe me, that was not a pretty picture.

"No way!" I shouted, and I backed away from the monster. As I did, it grew even bigger, until it seemed that the walls would split open.

This would have been a very good time for my dad to remember to come in and scold me for the whole flag incident, don't you think? Well, that didn't happen, though how the noise and the rumbling and the shaking floors could go unnoticed by two people who caught me bowling in my room because the falling pins woke them up I'll never know. The point is, no one came, so it was just me, Bigelow, and the monster toilet.

"Don't worry! I know just what to do!" Bigelow shouted, and ran past me and stood right in front of the monster. The monster leaned back and roared, then its jaws came flying forward and with one great snap, Bigelow was gone.

"Oh m-m-my..." I stuttered. "It...It *ate* him!"

A big grin spread across the toilet as it licked its lips, and then it turned back to me, eying me hungrily. I stumbled back as those dripping teeth came at me. The monster growled, and then lunged forward again, snapping at my legs. I dove back, but the monster drew

closer, until I was backed up against the wall. With no
retreat left, I gazed into the sneering eyes of the monster
as its gleaming teeth rose above my head...

Just then, Bigelow sprang out from behind the
monster! He hadn't been eaten, but had run past the
crashing jaws to my bed, and now he was running back
to me, carrying something in his hands.

"Here!" he shouted. "You need this!"

As he shoved it into my arms, I looked down to see what he had brought.

It was Teddy.

"What's *this* for?" I shouted, utterly bewildered. "Is he going to grow into a real bear and fight this thing?"

"Hold him!" Bigelow instructed. "Hug him!"

"Hug him? That's your great idea? You're telling me to fight for my life with a flashlight and a hug?"

But when you're desperate, you'll try anything, so I gave Teddy a squeeze. He felt so warm! I don't know how, but it soothed me a bit, in spite of the dreadful monster in front of me.

"That's it!" Bigelow shouted. "Now, use the light!"

As I clung tightly to Teddy, I turned back to face the monster. It glared at me with those hungry eyes and then reared back and roared ferociously. Somehow, though its roar struck me like a brick, the monster seemed a bit smaller than a moment ago. I pointed my flashlight right at it. The monster squinted, and squirmed, and then finally screamed as though it had been caught in flame rather than light. And then, amazingly, it began to shrink.

"That's it!" Bigelow shouted. "Don't stop now! You're doing it!"

I held the light steady, and as its fizzy beam rained down on the toilet, the monster kept getting smaller and smaller. When it was down to five feet tall, it began to cower, and then it retreated back toward the bed.

"Don't let it go back under!" Bigelow instructed. "Keep the light between the bed and the monster!"

I did as he told me, and backed the monster up into the corner of the room.

"Well done!" Bigelow exclaimed. "There's no escape now!"

The toilet kept getting smaller until it was only a few inches high. Then the shrinking stopped. It looked like a freaky happy meal toy.

"What happened?" I asked. "Why did it stop shrinking?"

"That's about as small as that one gets," Bigelow said.

"What? But then how do I get rid of it?"

"You don't," Bigelow explained. "It will be with you as long as it wants to be."

"What? You mean this monster could be with me *forever*?"

Right then I heard a noise: a gurgling, sloshing sound. I looked back at the monster.

"Oh... Oh NO!"

It was growing. In the few seconds it took for me to inhale a shaky breath, it was back to the size of a real, full-size toilet. And what was worse, I still had to pee.

"What help are you?" I shouted at Bigelow. "Look at that! What's to stop it from growing big again and eating me alive while I'm sleeping?"

"Use the RevealeR," Bigelow said calmly. "What do you see?"

I shivered, but squeezed Teddy even tighter, and then shined the light on the toilet.

"I see a monster," I said.

"Look again," he said. "Look harder."

In spite of my shivering, I gripped the flashlight tightly and moved in closer.

"I see..." I said, "I see..."

In the glow of my RevealeR's light, the eyes and teeth of the monster seemed to melt away.

"...I see a bowl made of clay, with a plastic seat on top and water running through it."

"That doesn't sound very frightening," Bigelow said. "Go on. Look *deeper.*"

Now, normally I prefer not to make a habit of looking at what's inside a toilet bowl, but this was sort of a special case, so I leaned in for a closer look.

"I see..." I tilted my head and squinted. "...I see an *image* inside. It looks like a little boy sitting on a toilet, crying for his mommy."

"Excellent!" Bigelow said. "What else?"

But right then, I stopped and straightened up.

"I don't need to look any more," I said, stepping back and turning to Bigelow. "I see it now. I finally see everything clearly."

I turned off the flashlight, but even without its beam washing over the monster, the gurgling sound was gone.

"It was *me*," I realized. "When I was three, I had to go to the bathroom in a department store, but the toilet was broken. It kept flushing while I was sitting on it. It was so loud! And I was afraid. Afraid that..."

"...That you would be sucked down the drain." Bigelow said.

"Yes."

"Turn the RevealeR back on," Bigelow instructed. "What does the light show you now?"

I turned on the light. Even in the dark, the monster had shrunk back to toy size. I studied it closely.

"What do you see?" Bigelow asked. "Anything that can hurt you?"

"No. I just see clay. Clay, and plastic, and water."

As I spoke, the monster grew smaller still. When it stopped shrinking this time, it was no bigger than a thimble. I picked it up. It snapped at me and tried to bite my finger, but its teeth were soft, and I didn't even feel it. It was like a dog trying to bite the wheel off a tank. I lifted my hand, with the monster still clinging to my finger with its gummy mouth, and swayed it back and forth.

"What do I do with it?" I asked.

"Put it on the shelf," Bigelow told me. "Just look at it once in a while, and it will never grow big again."

I walked over to my bookshelf, slid over a stack of mini-mysteries to make room, and squeezed the monster between the stack and a great big hardcover copy of the Baseball Records Book. The toilet's eyes scanned the huge towers of books surrounding it, and cringed.

"So, that's it?" I asked, wiping my hands together happily. Bigelow gave me a grim look.

"No, I'm afraid not," he said. I glared at him sourly.

"What? Why not? Did we take care of this monster or not?"

Bigelow scratched his head, doing that Jeannine-like scratch that he did.

"I think," he whispered, "there are more of them."

Chapter Six – The Truth Comes Out

"More?" I said nervously. Behind me, the toilet monster whimpered. "What...What makes you think so?"

"Well, for one thing, I saw several different monster trails when I looked under your bed."

I peeked under the bed myself, but saw only dust bunnies.

"I don't see any of that," I complained. Bigelow nodded, and pointed at his magnifying glass.

"That's what *this* is for," he told me. "It's called a MonsterScope. It helps me spot things that you can't see with your eyes alone."

"Oh. But how can you be sure that different trails means more than one monster? It could just be the same one making tracks on different nights."

Bigelow stiffened as though he was very offended.

"I am a Gold Shield Master Detective," he said huffily, pointing to the proud badge on his beat-up old coat.

"And an *expert* monster detective such as myself can tell the difference between the tracks of different kinds of monsters."

"How?"

"All monsters are different," he explained. "But they can be categorized. The two main categories are simple: smart monsters and dumb monsters. That toilet was a dumb monster. He growled and roared and flashed his teeth to scare you. He couldn't even talk."

"And smart monsters?"

"A smart monster wouldn't give himself away so easily. They're much better at hiding, usually behind some other monsters like this one."

"So," I reasoned, "You think that this monster was a decoy?"

Bigelow nodded.

"Or a pawn. You've been afraid of broken toilets since you were three. How long have you had a monster under your bed?"

I shrugged. "A few weeks, I guess."

"Then a few weeks ago, something must have happened. Something that...well, that created a monster that can open a doorway to your room. And he's shoving any other monster he can find through the door at you, so that he stays safely hidden, free to attack again and again."

Though I was terrified by what he told me, I couldn't help being very impressed.

"That's brilliant, Bigelow," I said. "You really are a great monster detective."

Bigelow shrugged modestly.

"I just know how they think," he said.

"Of course you do," I agreed. "After all, *you're one of them, aren't you*?!"

Bigelow froze.

"What...What makes you say that?" he stuttered.

"Oh come on, Bigelow," I insisted. "You just appear in my room from out of nowhere. You grow when I'm scared just like the toilet-monster did. My dad couldn't see you under the bed. Either you're not very smart, which you've already proven isn't true, or you've been purposely dropping clues all over the place. You *wanted* me to figure it out."

Bigelow broke into a sharp, toothy smile.

"You're a pretty good detective yourself," he said.

"Thanks. But what I don't understand," I went on, "is *why*."

"All monsters are different," he said again. "Those other monsters and I are different. We want different things."

I looked down into my arms.

"Teddy," I whispered, squeezing him tightly. "You want Teddy. But why?"

Bigelow stared at me, and his head swayed wistfully.

"How...how does it feel?" he asked, his gruff voice growing soft as a kitten's purr. "How do *you* feel when you hold him?"

"I feel...warm," I answered. "It feels like something is glowing inside me."

"That's it," Bigelow said. "I want to feel like that. That's what I want."

"Then what is it the others want?" I asked.

Bigelow straightened, then reached behind his back and pulled out an even bigger flashlight.

"That's what we have to find out," he said, and then he walked on over to the wall and flicked the switch, plunging the room back into darkness.

43

"Bigelow," I called out into the darkness. "How will I know when I've found him? The monster that's really behind it all, I mean."

"You'll know," Bigelow assured me. "You already know what he looks like."

"I do?"

I wondered what Bigelow meant by that, but before he could explain, the scratching sound reappeared. It didn't seem nearly as scary as the first time I'd heard it, but then it grew much louder and busier than before, as if a whole kennel of dogs was trying to dig its way in through the ceiling, walls, and floor. It echoed louder and louder until it was a thunderous roar. Bigelow grabbed my arm; his furry fingers were shaking uncontrollably.

"What's happening?" I asked.

"Uh, oh," Bigelow said weakly. "This is bad."

I turned to him and hollered, "This is bad? This is *bad?!* That is *not* what I want to hear right now, Bigelow!"

"He knows!" Bigelow screeched. "He knows we're on to him, so he's sending them all at us at once! Quick, turn on the light!"

I flicked the switch on my flashlight, but nothing happened. Again.

"Oh, no!" I shouted. "It's broken again! What do I do now, Bigelow?"

Bigelow didn't answer. I grabbed his shaking hand and pulled him toward me.

"Bigelow!" I shouted. But he was frozen in place. I could hear the scratching turn into a din of noises. There were roars, and screams, and crashes, and voices. And they were getting closer.

"Bigelow!" I pleaded. "Please, snap out of it!"

But he didn't move, or speak. He even stopped shaking. His arm was ice cold to my touch.

He...he's really frozen! He's actually scared stiff! I thought. And as the sounds of the monsters drew closer, I felt the cold grip of fear take hold of me as well. But even as the cold tried to fill me, I felt a surge of warmth flow into me from the arm that held tightly to my Teddy. I looked down at my bear, and then at Bigelow.

That's it! I realized. *I know what to do!*

"I know what you need, Bigelow!" I called out over the din. "Here, take this!"

And as the monsters drew near, I pressed Teddy into his hand. I thought that would revive him, but he remained frozen, and then the icy cold flooded my body as well.

Chapter Seven – The Hardest Part

For a moment, nothing happened, and I was sure I was about to end up as Monster Chow, but then the paw-like hand that held Teddy began to glow. Bigelow started to warm up, and then he swayed, stumbled a bit, and shook his head.

"W...What..." he mumbled. "What happened..."

"Never mind that!" I said. "They're here, Bigelow! They're *here*!"

Bigelow straightened, and then looked all around the pitch-black room. He cocked his head sideways as if he was listening intently to the symphony of monster sounds that filled the room, and sniffed at the air. His head spun quickly to the right, and then back to the left. Suddenly, his body stiffened, then he threw his shoulders back, handed Teddy back to me, and forcefully flicked on his flashlight. Slowly, he crept forward into the darkness.

"Hey! What about *me*?" I protested. Without a word, Bigelow reached back and put his furry hand on my flashlight, and it hummed back to life, lighting up brightly with a bubbly, greenish beam.

"Nice trick," I grumbled.

Bigelow ignored me. Instead, he pointed his light into the air around us. Scads of strange creatures flew in every direction, scattering as the light struck them.

"Bigelow, what are those things?"

But if Bigelow knew the answer, he didn't say. Instead, he continued to wave his light around the room. It looked like every inch of it was filled with creeping shadows that ran from the powerful beam.

"Don't get distracted!" he commanded. "Focus on the task at hand. We have to work together. I'll take care of the monsters on this side..." he pointed to his right. "...And you take those over there."

I turned to look where he had directed me, but all I saw was blackness. I pointed my light straight ahead, and then crept slowly forward into what seemed like a sea of ink. Suddenly, out of the darkened corner Bigelow had pointed at, a flash of giant, razor-sharp teeth snapped at my head, missing my face by inches.

"*Yeeeeiii!*" I screeched. "Bigelow, what *was* that?"

But there was no answer. Whatever it was shot through the air past me, and as it turned to make another pass, I caught sight of my attacker in the faint moonlight that fluttered in through my window. Right then, the air caught in my throat as though I had forgotten how to breathe.

"Sh-Sh-*Shark*!" I gasped.

For there, to my horror, was a giant bloodthirsty shark swimming *right through the air*. It came flying at me again with its red-stained jaws swiping in every direction.

"Bigelow!" I cried. "Bigelow, help!"

But in an instant, it was already upon me. I dodged just in time, and when the monster spun around for another try, I swung my flashlight around and caught it full in the face with the beam. The monster shark howled, began thrashing about like a harpooned whale, and then fell crashing to the floor. I kept the light on it as it lay there, shrinking it until it turned into a guppy that flopped around like...well, like a fish out of water.

"I did it!" I shouted. "Bigelow, I did it!"

"Good work!" Bigelow called out. "Now, put it on the shelf with the other one."

But before I could pick it up, a deep, heavy rumbling growled menacingly, echoing from every direction.

"What...what was that?" I wondered as I glanced nervously about. Just then, a crash of thunder shook the room like an earthquake, almost knocking me off my feet. I pointed my flashlight all around, scanning for the source, but before I could spot anything a blinding flash of lightning struck right at my feet, knocking me down.

"Yow! That was *close*!" I yelled. I tried to get up, but just as I lifted my head, another flash, like the beam from a ray-gun, erupted from above and whizzed past my face. I ducked, but from my knees I quickly pointed my flashlight up where the bolt had come from and caught the dark, churning mists of a monstrous storm in its beam. Hazy, venomous eyes scowled at me from the swirling blackness that hung overhead, even darker than a midnight sky, with its smoky fingers billowing across the ceiling.

"Gotcha!" I cheered.

A raging thunder shook the room, but the dark cloud, unable to escape the beam of my flashlight, slowly began to fade. The rumbling softened, until it was replaced by the splashing of a gentle spring rain. I actually smiled at that, until I saw that the rain that had fallen was being sucked up by huge, twisted roots that were covering the floor. My eyes followed the trail of roots to a hideously deformed monster tree, which grew so fast that in seconds it had spread across half the room. Before I could move, its branches reached out and wound themselves around me, pulling me toward a horrible, gaping maw in the trunk.

"NO!" I screamed. "LET ME GO!"

But with my hands bound by the rope-like vines, my flashlight was stuck pointing uselessly at the ceiling as I was drawn bit-by-bit into that horrible, slimy mouth. Its evil eyes glowered at me as my feet sank deep into that moss-covered maw, while I struggled and squirmed with all my might.

"Bigelow!" I shouted. "Bigelow, where are you?"

There were grunting and growling sounds coming from where Bigelow had stood, but I could not turn my head to see what was happening, so I fought on alone, twisting and pulling at the branches. But I just sank in deeper.

"SURRENDERRRR," hissed the monster tree. "GIVE IN TO YOUR FEARRR..."

"No Will!" I heard Bigelow shout. "Don't give up! The hardest part of any battle is to keep on trying when things look hopeless. But you can beat this thing if you just don't quit!"

I took heart from Bigelow's voice, but I still kept sinking. I was in almost up to my thighs when I heard a cracking sound: my twisting and tugging had finally split one of the vines that bound me.

"Yes!" I cried. "I did it!"

Before another vine could grab my arm, I tore my hand loose and pointed the light point-blank at the face of the tree. It groaned a weepy moaning sound, and my legs slid out of its mouth to the floor as the monster spat and retched violently.

"You think *I* taste bad?" I quipped. "Hah! You should try my mother's succotash casserole. *Nobody* can stomach *that*."

I kept the beam focused dead center on the trunk, which caused the tree to begin sprouting flowers all over its bare branches. Apparently, the monster tree found this very embarrassing, for it covered itself bashfully as it shrank, and then hopped away, owing to the lack of any legs, trying to escape. I was about to chase after it when I spotted Bigelow in the far corner beside my closet door. He was quite busy fending off both a giant spider and a dark, heavily wrinkled figure with oversized lips that looked very much like my Great Aunt Martha.

"No, this is no good!" he shouted. "There are too many of them! If you chase every one of these, you'll never uncover your Hidden Beast!"

"My *what*?"

"The monster behind it all! You must confront him!"

"Well then, what do I do?" I asked.

"Ignore these… these *secondary* monsters," Bigelow instructed. "Concentrate on finding the Hidden Beast!"

"How do I do that?" I shouted.

"Focus!" he yelled. "Something happened a few weeks ago. Something that set the beast free. What was it?"

I shuddered.

"I…I don't…remember…"

"Don't hide from it, Will!" Bigelow said. "Face it! Use the light!"

"N-No! I don't want to…"

But just then I heard voices. They emerged from the din and closed in around me, as though a crowd of people was approaching from all directions. Through the misty shadows, one voice came through much clearer, and closer than the others.

"Hey, pipsqueak!" It called to me with deep echoes floating all around. "What are you doing here?"

"He's here, Will!" Bigelow shouted. "Use the light!"

I slowly pointed the light in the direction of the voice. I expected some slimy creature with gruesome tentacles, hideous fangs, and flame for eyes, but it was something much worse. I started shaking when the light revealed a figure about five feet tall with stringy brown hair, a pale, acne-scarred complexion, and a huge hooked nose. He wore a beaten-up pair of jeans, unlaced sneakers, and a football jacket with the bold letter 'A' embroidered on the chest.

"It...It's just a *kid*!" Bigelow stammered.

"A really *big* kid," I said bitingly. Bigelow nodded knowingly.

"A bully," he said.

I nodded.

"But how do I make him go away?"

"Face him!" Bigelow yelled.

"But the light isn't working! He's not shrinking!"

"He is!" Bigelow insisted. "You just can't see it!"

"No! He's getting bigger!" I yelled.

"Face him!" Bigelow commanded.

"But I'm not big enough!" I cried.

"You are!" Bigelow called out. "You're big where it counts most! You trusted me, even though you knew I was a monster. You gave me Teddy when I needed him, even though *you* were afraid too. You *are* big, Will.

You're much bigger than him. Everything else is an illusion!"

I pointed the light at the bully. He didn't shrink.

"You can do it, Will!" Bigelow said.

I bit my trembling lip, and then shined the flashlight right into the monster's eyes. The bubbly stream of light seemed to bounce right off of his smug, *'I can get away with whatever I want'* grin.

"I-I'm not scared of you," I stuttered. But as my shaking fingers fought to hold steady the fizzy green beam from my RevealeR, the monster's face twisted into a warped, evil smile.

"Yes you are," he said, and then grew some more. "You're so scared you're gonna wet yourself."

Unfortunately, he was right. My knees were quaking and my heart pounded so hard that I could feel the pulse hammering in my ears. And as far as wetting myself...well, the less said about that the better.

"What do I do now, Bigelow?" I pleaded.

"Use the light," he said. "*Trust* the light. Look closer."

I don't know how I did it, but I stepped closer to the monster. My hands shook as I held the light up close to his face. Somehow, with the light shining on him, I saw something *behind* the monstrous smile. There was flicker of doubt, a twinge of...

"I *am* scared of you," I admitted. "But you...I see it now...*you're scared too!*"

As quickly as the words sprung from my mouth, his smile vanished. Tears began streaming down his face. I blinked, and saw that Bigelow was right: the monster *had* been shrinking. I just couldn't see it before.

"Why?" I asked the monster. "Why are *you* scared?"

The monster didn't speak. There, in the glare of the light, he became a boy barely bigger than me, cowering in a darkened room, alone but for the tiny flopping guppy that had fallen there earlier. Beside him lay a leather belt, and there were welts showing through the back of his shirt. He curled up and started whimpering, and I actually began to feel sorry for him. Just then, Bigelow stepped beside me.

"I'm afraid," he said, "That this one is going to hang around for quite a long time."

"That's okay," I said. "If I don't go in the water, the shark can't hurt me."

Bigelow's head shook, and I was sure this time that he rolled his eyes at me.

"I meant the *bully*," he said.

I looked down at Bigelow and smiled.

"So did I," I said. Bigelow smiled back at me. I turned back to the bully, but he was already gone.

"Hiding," Bigelow said. "That means the beast's last defense has fallen."

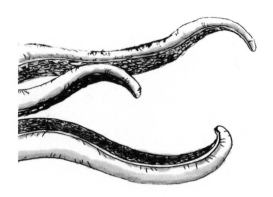

Chapter Eight – The Hidden Beast

I dropped my smile. It fell on the floor and scurried into the closet like a frightened hamster.

"What are you saying?" I sputtered. "Wasn't *that* the beast?"

"No," Bigelow said. "But he was the one who set the beast free."

"Then...then where is the..."

"Hush!" Bigelow cut me off, putting a hairy finger to his oversized lips. "Listen."

I pricked up my ears, and heard another voice emerge slowly, softly from the darkness. Though it was very faint at first, I recognized the voice instantly.

"**Will**," the voice called out.

I knew right then who it was, knew he was the beast.

"**Will**...**it's me**..."

"He's here, Will!" Bigelow shouted. "It's time! It's time to face him once and for all!"

"No..." I whimpered. "Oh, no...please..."

But from the black fog ahead, horrible tentacles shot out at me. I staggered back, and stumbled to the ground. I jumped right up and desperately fled, trying to escape.

"**Will, I**..."

"No!" I cried. "Leave me alone!"

But the monster did not leave me alone. Instead, flames suddenly burst from the darkness, driving me into a corner just as hideous claws leapt from the shadows and tried to rake at me.

"Use the RevealeR, Will!" Bigelow called out. "Point the light at the monster and face the truth about your fear!"

"No!" I shouted. "I don't want to! Just make it go away!"

But the monster kept advancing.

"**Will**," the monster's voice echoed. "**I**...**don't**..."

"Nooooo!" I pleaded, tears streaming down my face.

"**I**...**don't**...**love you**."

Backed into a corner with no hope of escape, I finally lifted my flashlight and shined its beam at the monster. The bubbles of light struck the tentacles and claws, washing them away like rain melting a sand castle. What finally remained, standing before me steady and unflinching in the glow of the light, was the Hidden Beast.

My father.

"Nooooo!" I moaned. I dropped the flashlight, and fell sobbing to the floor. "No, it's not true!"

"It's *not* true," Bigelow's steady voice called out. He shined his flashlight on the beast, who squinted, but held his ground.

"**I don't love you, Will**," the beast said, growing larger with each echo of my sobs.

"It's not true, Will!" Bigelow shouted. I lifted my head.

"It *is* true," I bawled. "I told my dad about the bully. I told him that I told a teacher, but the teacher didn't do anything! I told him it just wasn't fair! Do you know what he said to me? He said, '*The world's not fair, Will. Get used to it.*' Can you believe that?"

"Use your RevealeR, Will!" Bigelow shouted, "See the *whole* truth! The light from my RevealeR alone is not strong enough for this! We have to do it together!"

I stopped sobbing and looked up at the beast, who was now as big as a house. He looked so smug; it got me angry.

"Come on, Will! I know you have it in you!" Bigelow said.

I stared at the face of the beast, who looked down at me with the contempt my father had in his eyes the day he found out I'd quit pee-wee football. It was the scariest thing I'd ever seen.

"Think you're pretty tough, don't you?" I said fiercely. "You think you're so much stronger than I am! Well, surprise! I'm a lot stronger than you think! So take *this*!"

I picked up my flashlight and shined it in his face. Together with Bigelow's light, it made him cower.

"That's it!" Bigelow exclaimed. "That's it! Look at him! See the truth!"

And as I watched, the beast shuddered, and shook its head violently as though a bee had flown up its nose. Its temple began to swell, and the beast smacked it repeatedly until finally a *telephone* grew out of its ear. I don't think it liked having a phone stuck to its ear, because it scratched and clawed at it, but couldn't make it go away. Then a voice came out of the phone.

"I'm sorry, Mr. Allen," it said in a voice that sounded suspiciously like my principal, Ms. Greevey. It's a voice I remember well from the day I almost set the school's science lab on fire.

"Not sorry enough!" my father's voice shouted back. It was kind of funny, because the beast covered its mouth to try and keep the words from coming out, but I heard them loud and clear just the same.

"Not nearly as sorry as you *will* be," my father's voice continued, as the beast scratched and pulled at its own mouth to no avail. "Not as sorry as you're going to be if anything like this ever happens to my son again!"

"My dad did that?" I turned to Bigelow. "Why didn't he tell me?"

"Look some more," Bigelow urged. I turned back.

A chair had grown out of the beast's behind, growing larger as he shrank, until his feet were pushed out from under him and he was forced to sit. He looked like a three year old on a throne. The monster squirmed and struggled mightily to free himself, but then another voice spoke up and he grabbed at his mouth again. It was my mother's voice.

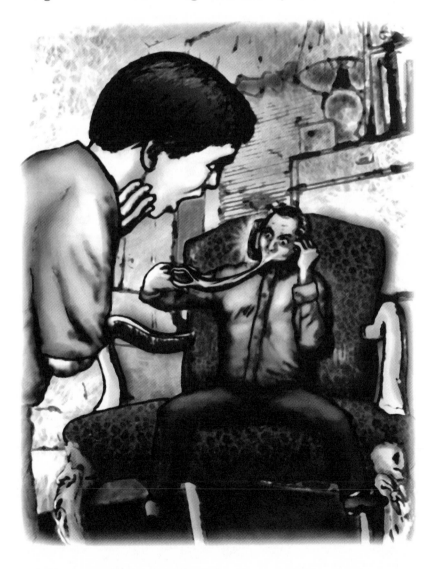

"Will it help?" she asked.

"I don't know," my father's voice answered. The beast pulled at its mouth and stretched it several feet off its face, but my father's voice still came out clearly.

"I don't know," he said despairingly. "They can't watch every bully every moment of the day in every inch of the school. But what else can we do?"

I stared hard at the monster, seeing him...*really* seeing him as I never had before.

"Daddy?" I said timidly as I stepped toward him. "Daddy...You...*You're scared too*?"

The phone and the chair melted. The beast tried to put its mouth back into place, but it was hopelessly stretched. I stepped right up to it and shined the light on its face. It shrunk down to...well, *daddy* size. Just the right size to do what needed to be done. Somehow, I knew exactly what that was.

"That's it," Bigelow urged. "Go on..."

I stepped forward and gave the beast a great big hug.

"**Nooooo!**" it cried out, and began shaking all over. I let go of the beast and stepped back. It shook, and rattled, and then split open in several places. Light poured out of the cracks, and the beast tried desperately to hold itself together, but the fissures kept yawning wider. Finally there was a gigantic explosion, filling the room like the sun, wiping away the beast and all of the remaining monsters in one great burst of light. When the glow faded, all that remained was Bigelow, me, and some weird new happy meal sized toys together in a darkened room.

"That was him?" I concluded. "That was my big, horrible monster?"

"Yes," Bigelow said.

I smirked, and wiped my hands contentedly.

"What a wimp," I snickered. Bigelow chuckled.

"So," I asked. "Is it over now?"

"Almost. You still have one more monster to face."

Chapter Nine – The Final Monster

"Bigelow, do you mean...you?" I asked. "I have to face *you*?"

"Yes. You recognize me now, don't you, Will?"

"N...No, I don't."

"You do." Bigelow insisted.

I looked down and turned away.

"But I don't want *you* to go away," I said quietly.

"I won't," he assured me. "I promise."

Just then, my eyes caught sight of Teddy, and I realized that I had been squeezing him tightly in one arm all this time.

"It looks like he's been squeezed like that a lot," Bigelow observed.

"Yes," I told him. "He always made me feel safe when I was scared. I used to take him everywhere. But then..."

I trailed off. I remembered what had happened, and I started getting very upset.

"I...I lost him. We were on vacation, and I lost him. I was afraid I would never see him again."

As I said this, Bigelow grew. In just a few seconds, the trench coat wasn't dragging on the floor anymore, and long, hairy arms were coming out of the sleeves.

"But then we found him!" I cried out. "We found him! I hugged him so hard. I wouldn't let go of him the whole trip home, and then I brought him back up to my room. I've never taken him out of my room since."

I looked up at Bigelow. His fingers had become long talons, and his teeth were now fangs as big as daggers.

"You're still growing," I said.

"**Yes**," Bigelow answered in a low, raspy growl.

I looked down at Teddy, and gave him a great, big hug.

"I love you, Teddy," I told him as I squeezed him hard. Then I turned to Bigelow. He was huge now, standing almost from floor to ceiling, with thick, fur-covered legs showing beneath his coat.

"Here," I said as I put Teddy in those great, hairy arms. "He's yours now. Take good care of him."

And that's when the most amazing thing happened. Bigelow looked at me and smiled, with his giant, razor sharp teeth shining out from his crescent shaped, ear-to-ear mouth. And he started to glow. He glowed brighter and brighter, and as he shone, he shrank. By the time the glow faded, he was back to his original size.

"You're looking better," I told him. He smiled.

"So are you," he said.

I smiled too. It was the biggest smile I ever smiled.

"You'll be okay now," he said. "None of these monsters will bother you anymore."

"All thanks to you," I said gratefully. "You really are a great monster detective."

"So are you," he said. "You know, the monster detective business is very short-handed at the moment. Maybe you could help out."

"But...but I'm not a monster," I reminded him.

"Oh, that's not what your mother says," Bigelow answered. But then he broke out into a big smile to show me that he was joking.

I think.

"Anyway, you're smart, and brave, and you know what to do now. That should be enough."

"But how will people find me? *You* at least have a business card."

"Now you do too," he said. "Just look."

I reached into my pocket and took out Bigelow's card. It now read:

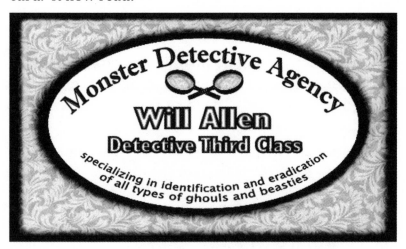

I looked back at Bigelow, who still wore that great big smile. He handed me a magnifying glass and a silver badge. The glass, like Bigelow's, had a faint greenish aura surrounding it. I lifted it and used it to look all over my room. When I turned to my shelf, the tiny toilet monster sitting there glowed eerily through the lens.

"Wow!" I cheered. "My very own monster spyglass!"

"*MonsterScope*," Bigelow corrected. "It's called a MonsterScope. That, the RevealeR, and your own wits and bravery are the only tools you need to do the job."

"Well, thanks," I said, lowering the glass. "I just hope I don't have to get paid in teddy bears."

"That reminds me," Bigelow said. "Look."

He pointed at my bed. There, sitting next to the pillow, was Teddy. This time I was *sure* that he was smiling too.

"How did he get...But...but Bigelow, he's yours now," I protested. "You earned him fair and square."

"Yes I did," he agreed. "We should always earn our friends. And keep on earning them. Remember I promised you that I would give him a home where he would always be happy?"

I nodded.

"Well, I can think of no place in the world where my friend Teddy would be happier than right there on your bed. Just as long as he gets to come with me on an adventure now and then."

I rushed up and gave Bigelow a big hug. He seemed to like it, even if it did make him shrink some more.

"MMMERRFF...Easy...does...it..." he managed to get out in a muffled voice. I let him go and stepped back.

"Sorry," I said. "It looks like I made you even smaller."

"Just remember," Bigelow said, "Size isn't everything. A little person..."

"Can solve some really big cases," I finished. He smiled again.

"And you are very big where it counts most," he told me, and then turned to my bed. He leaned over and stuck his head underneath, but then looked back, gave me a playful wink, and climbed on top and crawled under the covers. There, beside his new friend Teddy, he formed a great lump that gradually shrank, until the blanket lay flat on the bed. Teddy smiled happily, feeling that his new friend, though unseen, was still there beside him.

"Everything else is just an illusion," I recalled. Then I put out the light and climbed into bed.

Chapter 10 - Beginnings

The next morning, I got out of bed, gave Teddy a hug, and went and checked the shelf. There, sitting among my books, camera, and baseball glove were a plastic guppy, a two-inch tall tree that cowered shyly, and a tiny toy toilet with the personality of a snapping turtle.

"Good morning, fellas," I said. "How are you doing today?"

None of them seemed at all pleased. Maybe one day they would get tired of hanging around, but until then, I thought I might get a terrarium for them or something. If I figured out what to feed them, they would make very interesting pets.

On the way out of the kitchen after breakfast, I surprised my mom and dad by giving them each a big hug. Once they got over the shock, they seemed to like it, even though it made my dad gag on his scrambled eggs a little. Or maybe that was because there was something hard and chunky in them again. With my mom's cooking, you can never be sure. Anyway, I met up with Jeannine on the ride to school and told her all about what happened the night before. She seemed a little skeptical, until I showed her my new business card and silver badge.

"Monster detective!" she exclaimed. "You, Will, a monster detective! Oh, I'm so jealous!"

"Don't be," I said. "You can be my partner."

Jeannine turned red. Her mother was right: it's not her color.

"Oh, Will! Do you mean it?" she practically gushed. "Me, your partner?"

"Sure," I said. "Sherlock Holmes has Dr. Watson, doesn't he? All detectives have partners. Or secretaries, at least."

"Oh, this will be so great!" she said. "You can do the snooping and the fighting monsters stuff, and I can..."

Her smile faded a bit.

"Um, what exactly *can* I do?"

"Well, you can do the case logs," I suggested. "And the research. You're aces at that. There's lots of stuff to look up when you run a detective business, I'll bet. And you can handle publicity. You're much better at talking to people than I am."

Jeannine smiled at that, but then it faded again.

"You know Will," she said. "now that I think about it, how are we going to find any clients? Are we going to advertise or something?"

I stopped and thought that over for a minute.

"Hmmm," I finally said. "I don't think so. I think we'll be better off keeping this whole thing a secret. After all, this *is* middle school. If word gets around, we'll have a lot of people making fun of us all the time. Who wants that?"

Jeannine started scratching her head.

"Well then, what do we do?" she said.

Just then, there was some rustling in the aisle as a boy I'd never seen before crept up and crouched beside us. Jeannine and I both quickly froze. At first his eyes darted about nervously, but then he looked right at me.

"Will Allen?" he said.

I turned and looked over at him. Even though he was crouching, it was clear that he was a whole lot taller than either me or Jeannine, with long red hair and very big, round glasses.

"Yes, that's me," I answered.

"Are... are you really Will Allen, the monster detective?" he asked.

Jeannine and I turned to each other. She looked just as shocked as I did.

"Who wants to know?" I asked suspiciously.

"My name's Timmy. Timmy Newsome. I need your help." He looked around, and then leaned in very close and whispered, "I have a monster in my closet."

I looked at Jeannine, and then back at Timmy and asked, "How did you find me?"

"Well, I don't know how it got there," he said. "But your business card was in my backpack this morning."

He handed it to me, and when I saw what was on it, my mouth fell open, which was sort of a bad thing to have happen, since my gum fell out onto the floor of the bus. I passed the card over to Jeannine, whose eyes grew wide as she read:

Jeannine and I looked at each other and smiled.

"So," I said to Timmy. "What's eating you?"

That's a little monster detective joke.

Okay, a *very* little monster detective joke.

But then, it's not so bad to be very little, is it? After all, a little person can solve some really big cases.

So that's how it all began. But if you think things got easy after that, think again. In fact, before I even began investigating my first case, I discovered that being a detective was going to be a lot tougher than I thought.

Chapter Eleven – Introductions

First of all, let me tell you that starting your own business is not easy. It's a lot of work, not the least of which is trying to convince your parents that you have to be allowed to stay out past your bedtime to do your job. It's one of the many complications you face when you're starting up a monster detective agency.

"Don't miss your curfew tonight," my mother warned in her *'or you'll be in big trouble'* tone of voice as I tip-toed across the hallway to our front door. I froze in my tracks, and looked toward the kitchen to find her staring down at me.

"How did you..." I began, but my mom cut me off.

"And what in the world are you doing in those ratty old clothes?" she asked, eyeing the trench coat and bowler hat that I'd stolen out of the attic with a look of disgust on her face.

"It's my uniform," I replied, pointing at the silver medallion pinned on my coat. "Can't you read my badge? It says: Monster Detective Agency, Detective

Third Class! I'm on my way to Timmy Newsome's house to solve my very first..."

"Never mind!" my mother interrupted curtly. "Just make sure you're home by eight o'clock."

"*Eight* o'clock? Mom, I'm in middle school now!"

"Eight o'clock, or you'll be grounded for a week."

I frowned. Since Bigelow told me that monsters don't come out during the daytime, I knew I'd have to wait until dark to get started, so it was a pretty sure thing that I would end up being late.

"But mom," I protested. "I might not be finished doing my...you know, my *job* by then."

That put her in a bit of a snit.

"Your silly charade will be over when I say so," she hissed.

Mothers just don't understand free enterprise.

"That's not fair!" I complained. "You don't punish dad when *he* has to work late."

For some reason, she grinned slyly at that.

"Oh, you think so?" she said.

Now as any kid knows, arguing with a mom is totally useless. Especially when she's dead wrong about something. Of course, that never stopped me before, but I had a job to get to, and time was wasting, so I gave in.

I really hate doing that.

"Fine," I grumbled through gritted teeth. "Eight o'clock."

My mother smiled smugly, which just made it worse. I reached into my pocket and pulled out the special RevealeR flashlight that Bigelow had given me, but when I pointed it at my mother and flicked the switch, the light that came out was... well, *normal,* and it had no effect.

"Well, this really stinks!" I grumbled to myself. "What good is a monster-fighting flashlight that won't work on *moms*?"

"What was that?" my mom asked.

"Ah, nothing," I said, thinking as I did that the next time I had a job, I'd tell my mom I was going for a sleepover.

It was already dusk when I left the house. The little color that was left on the autumn leaves still clinging to their branches had faded into a strange, murky mist that drifted menacingly through the trees. Bits of that eerie fog reached out in all directions like fingers looking for something to strangle.

You know, spooky stuff like that used to make my hair stand on end like a cat that had its tail stepped on, but now that I know that there really are monsters out there, it doesn't bother me at all.

Don't ask me to explain it: I'm a detective, not a psychiatrist.

"Silly charade!" I growled into the syrupy air as I walked to Timmy Newsome's house. "She called it a silly charade! I'd like to see *her* face a monster or two! Then let's see what she called it!"

Of course, I knew that was impossible. After all, Bigelow told me that grownups can't even *see* kids' monsters because they are scared of different things than us. Personally, I don't think that my mother could see one unless it looked like a dent in the fender of her car, or a big stain in the middle of her Persian Rug.

That dark, swirling mist seemed to follow me every step of the way to Timmy's house. It swallowed the stars, the moon, and the light from the streetlamps as it crept across the sky, and spat out a shadowy haze all around me.

"13...15...17..." I counted as I passed each mailbox. "Ah, here we are! 23 Secor Lane."

I looked up from the mailbox to see Timmy's house, which was glowing darkly in the light of the hazy cloud. It was bigger than my house, with a huge terrace hanging out over the driveway of the two-car garage, and was surrounded by large, untrimmed hedges. The outer walls were covered in climbing vines, and the grounds were bordered by a white picket fence with faded, peeling paint. The gloomy cloud overhead fell across the cracked stone path leading to the front door and perched itself along the crown of the house as I approached. It would be hard to explain how, but I could *feel* that there was something evil lurking in that house. I took a deep breath and boldly stepped through the gate, which creaked loudly as it opened, but I was still shooting an occasional glance up at the shadows swirling above me as I stepped onto the portico and rang the bell. A woman with an upturned nose and hair pasted with enough gel to hold back a rhino answered the door. Her frozen scowl and perfectly manicured claw-like nails reminded me a little bit of my great aunt Martha, and a little bit of a pterodactyl.

"Yes?" she said, eyeing me like I was a load of toxic waste dumped on her doorstep.

"I'm Will Allen," I answered in my most professional tone of voice. "I'm here to help Timmy with his..."

"...My math homework!" Timmy shouted as he dashed down the stairs in our direction. He stopped at the door and bent over, panting. His long red hair spilled over his big, round glasses, making him look a lot like Poindexter from the Rocky and Bullwinkle Show.

No, I'm not making that up. If you've never heard of him, you haven't been watching the Classic Cartoon Channel.

"Will's a whiz at math, mom," he said breathlessly.

I fixed him with one of my patented '*say what?*' looks. I mean, I *am* a whiz at math, but I don't think that's likely to be very helpful when dealing with some giant, slobbering squid, saber-toothed purple gorilla, or whatever it was that might be lurking in Timmy's room.

"Oh! Well, do come in," his mother said in a suddenly gracious tone. Her scowl eased, but the frown lines remained etched in her face. Timmy ushered me quickly through the foyer and up the stairs to his room.

"We'll be working in my room, mom," he called out as he shoved me through the door. "Tell dad that's where I'll be."

"Timmy," his mother called back in a strangely exasperated voice, "You know your father..."

But Timmy slammed the door before she could finish. He looked up at me nervously as I scanned all around his room. There was nothing clearly monstrous about it, unless you count the fact that it was unnaturally clean and tidy, but it was definitely not a normal-looking kid's room either. The furniture and decorations were all old, antique stuff, like they came from a museum or something. The desk, dressers, and most everything else were made of dark, brown wood that was grainy and coarse. As I scanned the walls, I noticed that they were lined with lots of fancy, framed pictures, but none of them were of Timmy. Along the far wall was a roll-top desk with lots of drawers labeled with strange words on them, and a matching end table with a phone on top was sitting in the corner near the closet door. Sticking out into the middle of the room from the wall opposite the closet was a big four-post bed with a canopy on top. To look at this room, you'd think that it was the guest room at a fancy inn, not the home of a twelve year old boy.

"So," Timmy said, leaning in close enough for me to smell the onions on his breath, "Do you really think you can help me?"

"If you can handle your monster as rough as you did me," I answered tartly, shoving him away, "you won't *need* any help."

You have to understand: I was upset because being shoved around by people bigger than me has always been one of my worst nightmares. Mind you, it's not that I haven't come to expect that sort of thing, what with being one of the smallest kids in school, but now that I'd conquered my fears I certainly wasn't going to put up with being treated that way anymore, especially by someone who was begging me for help. Timmy, who stood nearly a head taller than me, backed away and bit his lip.

"Look, I'm sorry about that, okay?" he said. "I just don't want my mom to know what's going on."

"Why not?"

"Because..." he sputtered, "because she thinks it's all a dream or something. First she took away all my comic books because she said they must be causing me nightmares. Then she sent me to a *shrink*!"

"A what?"

"A psychiatrist! She doesn't understand. My monster is *real*. Who knows what she'll do if she finds out what you're really here for?"

"So you told your parents that I'm a...a math tutor?"

"Yes!" he said, grabbing my shirt urgently. "So, can you help me or not?"

I pulled myself out of his grip.

"Relax," I told him. "If I couldn't help, my card wouldn't have appeared in your book bag."

"That reminds me," he said, scratching his head just like Jeannine always does. "I was meaning to ask you: how did you do that? How did you put that card in my bag without me seeing you? And for that matter, how did you even know I have a monster?"

"I *didn't* know," I explained. "But the *card* did."

Timmy gave me a squinty kind of look. He reached into his pocket and pulled out a small rectangle of paper that I instantly recognized was my special business card. He looked at it up and down with the same squinty look.

"I don't get it," he finally said.

"Actually, neither do I," I answered. "Come on, let's get to work."

Chapter Twelve – Echoes

The clock ticked loudly as we both stood silently in the middle of Timmy's room. That throbbing beat rebounded off of every wall, and seemed to get louder with each echo.

"Well?" Timmy finally blurted.

I squirmed a little. To be perfectly honest, now that the time had come to begin my very first investigation, I felt a bit nervous. Fortunately, one thing I know for sure is that the secret to being a professional is to always act like you know what you're doing, even if you're clueless. I learned that from all the times I've seen my dad nod his head stupidly while his auto mechanic blabs a lot of gibberish at him.

"Okay," I squeaked. I coughed, and then started again in a deliberately deep voice.

"Okay, the...um...the first thing we need to do is figure out what makes the monster appear," I said.

"Great," Timmy replied. "And *how* do exactly are we going to do that?"

Um, I'm not really sure, I thought. But I wasn't going to tell Timmy that, so I bit my lip and fidgeted a bit, until finally an idea came to me.

Just do all the same things Bigelow did, I reasoned. *After all, it worked pretty well on MY monsters.*

So I tried to do exactly what Bigelow had done when he first appeared. First, I pulled out the special flashlight and magnifying glass that Bigelow had given me, then I went to the light switch and turned it off. The room went dark, but some hazy moonlight filtered in through the mist surrounding the windows and gave everything around us an eerie blue glow.

"What did you do that for?" Timmy cried, his voice suddenly tense.

"We need for it to be dark," I explained. "That's the only way to lure out your monster."

"Then what's the flashlight for?" he asked.

"This flashlight is special," I said, holding it up for him to see. The weathered red casing gleamed in the hazy light. "It's called a RevealeR. It can shrink your monster until it's too small to scare you anymore."

Now, I expected to hear a '*WOW*' or maybe a '*Really? That's amazing!*'

"Oh," was all he said. I looked at him, waiting for anything else to come out of his mouth, but he just shifted his gaze nervously around the room.

"So, where does the monster come at you from?" I finally asked.

"Over there," he answered, pointing to the corner of his room. There stood the closet door, and beside it the small end table with a telephone sitting on top. "They come out of the closet over there."

"I'll go check it out," I said boldly. I walked on over, my magnifying glass pressed to my face, searching for signs of monsters. Inch by inch I crept, flashlight at the ready, to the closet door. There was no sign of anything strange in the sight of the glass, but the air became stale with the odor of rotting fish. The smell grew more and more foul with every step I took. That made me edgy.

"I...I'm going in," I announced, and gently prodded the door.

Before I could even gasp, it flew open with a loud, creaking howl, and something dark and slimy fell upon me.

"YYYYYAAAAAAHH!" I screeched.

"YYYYEEEEAAAAAHH!" Timmy echoed

"OH MY GOD!" I shouted. "IT...IT'S SO HORRIBLE!"

"What is it?" Timmy cried. "What do you see?"

"What a mess!" I exclaimed, holding my nose as I gingerly lifted something that looked like a bunch of rotting banana peels off my coat. "And what a stink! Have you been using your closet as a trash bin?"

"It's the monster, you jerk!" Timmy bellowed.

"I don't think so," I shot back, examining the slimy mess carefully. "This is disgusting, but it's no monster. In fact, I don't see any monsters in here at all. No monster tracks, either."

"How can you see that?" Timmy asked.

"This isn't some plain old magnifying glass," I explained as I dropped the putrid scraps back into Timmy's closet, "It's a MonsterScope. It lets me see stuff you can't see with just your eyes. *Monster* stuff, you know? Monster trails, footprints – things like that. But there's none of that in there. So, what's the deal?"

"Huh?" Timmy sputtered. "What do you mean?"

"I mean why am I looking at a closet full of rotting food that has no monster in it?"

"There *is* a monster," Timmy insisted. "There is!"

"I know that," I told him. "If there wasn't, you wouldn't have gotten my card. But what's all this mess about? *Really*?!"

I held my MonsterScope up and looked at him through it. The strange aura surrounding the glass must have spooked Timmy, because he suddenly cowered shyly as though he thought that my scope could tell whether he was lying or not.

It can't, but of course Timmy didn't know that.

"All right, all right! I threw that stuff in there to feed the monster so it wouldn't eat me," Timmy confessed.

I turned back to the closet and looked over the rotting scraps with my MonsterScope, but they had no glowing tracks or prints on them.

"It doesn't look as though it likes what's on your menu," I commented. "I guess your monster is a fussy eater."

Timmy threw his hands up in the air.

"Well then, what *does* it want?" he whined.

"I don't know," I answered. "That's what we need to find out."

I put away my flashlight and began scanning with my MonsterScope, making a big, sweeping circle that started at the closet door and went all around the room.

Nothing.

"It might help me know what to look for," I suggested, "if you tell me more about the monster itself."

"Like what?" Timmy asked.

I tried to remember the questions Bigelow had asked me when he was searching for my monster. I began by asking, "What do you see?" but Timmy just said, "Nothing, really. Just things moving around in the shadows sometimes. Mostly, I hear it."

"You hear it? Does it *say* anything?"

Now that might seem like a pretty simple question to you, but Timmy acted like I'd just asked if he still wore plastic undershorts.

"No!" Timmy yelled, suddenly enraged. "No it doesn't say anything! Just stop it! You're not helping!"

He looked so angry that I thought he might explode, but just then the phone on the end table rang, and he froze like a stone.

"Aren't you going to get that?" I asked.

Timmy didn't answer. He just stood there as the phone kept ringing. And ringing.

And ringing some more. I don't know how many rings it took before it occurred to me that there was something suspicious about it, but I decided to check it out.

I walked back over to the end table and bent down to look at the phone more closely. To the naked eye, it appeared to be perfectly normal, but when I held my MonsterScope up and peered through the glistening glass, the receiver lit up with dozens of glowing spots.

"Yes! This is it!" I whispered excitedly. "Monster trails!"

"Timmy, I've found something!" I yelled. "I've found traces of the monster!"

"No! No you haven't!" he cried. "You haven't found *anything*! This isn't doing any good! Go get my dad! He's the only one who can help me!"

"But I..." I stammered.

"Stop it!" Timmy screamed. "Just stop what you're doing and leave me alone!"

At this point, I was feeling a bit unappreciated. But I went to that room to be a monster detective, and a monster detective doesn't give up, even when his client is even weirder than any monster. I was determined to do my job, so I pulled my special flashlight back out and pointed it at the phone.

"We should see where these trails lead..." I insisted.

But when I flicked the switch on the RevealeR, nothing happened.

"Uh oh. This is bad..." I mumbled, smacking the casing with my hand.

"You see!" Timmy shouted. "You're useless! Now just get out!"

"But the ringing..."

"Never you mind about the ring! That's none of your business, so stay out of it!"

As far as I was concerned, this whole thing was getting a little freaky, even by monster detective standards.

"I didn't say *ring*. I said *ringing*," I bellowed. "Aren't we going to do something about..."

But then I stopped speaking, because next to the phone I suddenly spotted the glint of a shimmering... *something.* I stepped around the end table for a better look, and there, on the other side of the phone, sat a glistening golden ring.

"Wha...?" I mumbled to myself. "But...but that wasn't there a second ago."

Now, you don't have to be a genius or a monster detective to know that there's something strange about things that just appear from out of nowhere. So, naturally, I moved in close and held my MonsterScope up to check it out.

"Wha...What are you doing?" Timmy whispered nervously. "Stop! Stop that!"

Through the glass, the ring lit up brightly with a kaleidoscope of colors and images. A sparkling steam arose from all around the golden band, which throbbed with hidden power.

"This..." I realized, "This is *it*! This is the monster!"

I smiled broadly, beaming with pride.

I've done it! I thought joyfully. *All on my own, I've detected a monster!*

But as I stared at the glowing band, my smile faded. I was actually kind of disappointed. After all, after facing creatures like a giant flying shark, a humongous monster tree, and a ten-foot-tall man-eating toilet, this tiny little thing was something of a letdown.

What am I going to do? I thought morosely as I picked up the ring and looked it over. *There's not much point in trying to shrink this thing.*

Just then, the phone rang again. Except it wasn't the phone at all. With the ring held tight in my fingers, I could feel the band vibrate and shake as the sound emerged. The ringing was coming from *it*, not the phone.

"Well, this is annoying," I grumbled. I turned back to Timmy, who recoiled like he had seen a...

...Well, something a lot scarier than a tiny little ring.

"This is it?" I asked, holding up the ring to Timmy's face. "*This* is your terrifying monster?"

Timmy stumbled back like I was trying to feed him castor oil.

"Shut up!" he shrieked. "Shut up and go away!"

"But I..."

"I mean it!" Timmy insisted. "Get out and leave me alone!"

For some reason, it seemed like a bad time to point out that I hadn't been paid yet. With my flashlight dead, and faced with a tiny little monster that did nothing but sit around making an annoying ringing sound, it didn't seem like there was much I could do anyway. I put the ring back down on the table and headed for the door, thinking as I did that at least I would be home in time for my curfew.

Chapter Thirteen - Enlightenment

By the time I got back to my room I was feeling pretty irritated, especially since my dad's first words when I came in the door were, "So, how did it go tonight, detective boy? Did you catch us a big, bad monster?"

I don't know which was worse, my mother calling my profession a silly charade, or my dad trying to humor me. I grumbled something a little bit like, "detect *this*," as I stormed up the stairs. My dad called after me.

"I'm sorry," he bellowed, "but I couldn't quite make that out. Would it help if I got an English-Monster Language translator?"

Okay, I was wrong. I *do* know which was worse.

I slammed my door shut and plopped down in my chair. My foul mood grew as I took out my flashlight and looked it over. I flicked the switch back and forth, but nothing happened.

"Maybe the batteries are dead," I said to myself.

Hey, I'm not a detective for nothing. I opened the battery compartment, and my jaw dropped.

There were no batteries at all.

"No wonder!" I sputtered. "Well, this should be easy to fix. I wonder if it takes AAs?"

"Not exactly," spoke a squeaky, yet gravelly voice.

I turned my head in the direction of the voice, which had come from an empty spot on my bed next to where my teddy bear sits. As I watched, a bulge began to form under my blanket, which grew taller until it rose about three feet off my bed. From within, something tugged at the blanket, but since he had been standing on it, the blanket pulled his feet out from under him and the blanket-wrapped figure toppled over.

"Wooooff!" he coughed when he smacked into the floor with a thud. "Stupid blanket!"

I could see flailing and scratching going on underneath, so I yanked my blanket off the figure before it ended up torn to shreds. There, sprawled on the floor before me, was the Great Monster Detective, Bigelow Hawkins. He righted himself, ruffled his huge trench coat, and straightened his bowler hat.

"Hello, Will," He said cheerfully. "How's tricks?"

I was still in a sour mood from Timmy kicking me out and my dad making fun of me, so I replied rather crossly, "How's *tricks*? Is that supposed to be funny?"

"Sorry," he said, backing away. "It's just a routine monster greeting."

"I...I'm sorry, Bigelow," I said. "I didn't mean to be cranky with you. It's just that I'm having a really rough night. I don't feel like a very good detective right now. Maybe I'm not cut out for this after all."

"Don't worry, Will. The first time is always the toughest. You'll get the hang of it."

"You really think so?"

"Of course! And I'm here to help," he announced eagerly. "So, what's the problem?"

"Well, for starters, *this*," I said, shoving the flashlight at him. "This stupid flashlight!"

"You mean your RevealeR?" Bigelow corrected.

"Whatever you call it!" I grumbled. "But I can't get it to work!"

"Yes you can," Bigelow insisted. "It's just that it doesn't work simply because you want it to."

My cheeks flared heatedly (as usual) and my hands molded into clubs. I bit my lip and then growled, "Bigelow, would you mind not speaking in riddles?"

"It's not a riddle," he maintained. "Can you tell me what the RevealeR does?"

94

"It..." I hesitated. "It shines light on monsters. It shrinks them until they can't hurt us anymore."

"Yes, of course," Bigelow agreed. "But there is more to it than that. What does the light actually *do* to the monsters that causes them to shrink?"

I thought back, remembering how my monsters had changed before my eyes when Bigelow shined the light from his RevealeR on them.

"It reveals the truth about the monsters," I whispered. "It shows them for what they really are, and makes them less scary."

"Very good, Will. Now, seeing the truth about monsters, or anything else for that matter, takes understanding. The light of understanding is one of the most powerful forces in the whole universe. But where do you suppose the power that creates a light like that comes from?"

I thought that over for a moment, remembering the empty battery compartment. I looked down at my flashlight, which was warm and glowing in my hand.

"It...it comes from *me*," I said, looking back up at Bigelow. "That's it, isn't it? It comes from inside me."

"That's right," Bigelow encouraged. "Go on."

"So if I don't understand the monster," I reasoned, "then I have no light to shine on it?"

"Exactly," Bigelow said. "So you see, the flashlight itself always works. But you need understanding..."

"...To make it light," I finished for him.

"You see?" he said with a smile. "You really *are* a good detective."

But there was something else, something that had been nagging at me since Timmy brought it up back in his room.

"Bigelow, why did my business card show up in Timmy's book bag? How does it work?"

"You're a monster detective now," Bigelow reminded. "It works the same for you as it did for me."

"It just appears to those who need my help?" I asked.

"Of course," Bigelow confirmed. "The card appears when someone has a monster and they are ready for you to help them."

"But then why couldn't I help Timmy?"

"Don't worry," Bigelow smiled. "You will."

"How? Tell me what to do!" I pleaded.

Bigelow scratched his head, and I wondered to myself why, except for me, thinking makes everyone's head itch. Maybe it's because they're all allergic to it.

"There's only so much I can tell you," Bigelow explained. "And you already know most of it."

"Can't tell me more?" I complained. "Why? Are there monster lawyers out there checking up on you?"

"Oh, no," Bigelow mused. "No, we killed all of those."

I'm *pretty* sure he was joking.

"No," he continued, "the reason I can't explain more is because there is no more to explain. You see, Will, every room, every monster, has its own set of rules, and it's up to you, the detective, to figure them out."

"So I have to figure out why a phone and a ring are Timmy's monsters," I reasoned. "Then my RevealeR can show the truth to Timmy, and make them less scary."

Bigelow beamed.

"But what could be so terrifying about a tiny little ring?" I puzzled.

"That's what you have to figure out," Bigelow said. "When you do, your flashlight will be able to reveal the truth about Timmy's monster. The light of understanding will show you what it really is, and Timmy will be able to see it too. If he wants to."

"If he *wants* to?"

"Of course," Bigelow said. "You can't simply show Timmy the truth about the monster. It's not enough that he *can* see the truth. He has to *choose* to see it. And you must help him make that choice. Until Timmy chooses to face them, the monsters will just grow stronger."

"You mean..." I said hesitantly, "*I* can't fight them?"

"No, Will," Bigelow answered. "You're a detective, not a soldier. You can only act as a guide. The only one who can defeat Timmy's monsters is Timmy himself."

"What if Timmy doesn't face them?" I asked nervously. "Could they grow big enough to...you know...devour us alive?"

"Monsters don't consume flesh," Bigelow explained, sounding strangely annoyed. "They live by consuming something much more powerful than that. Something so strong that it can crush the will of the strongest men and paralyze entire armies in its devastating grip."

"Fear," I concluded. "They feed on our fears, don't they? That's why mine grew when I was afraid."

"Very good, Will," Bigelow said.

"But then wouldn't it be doubly frightening," I posed, "if a monster dispatched the fearless detective in some gruesome way right before Timmy's eyes?"

Bigelow seemed to be caught by surprise by that question.

"That won't happen," he said, but his squeaky voice sounded tense. "Don't worry, Will. If Timmy wasn't ready to face his monsters, the card wouldn't have appeared to him."

I wasn't convinced. But then Bigelow hadn't been in that room with Timmy, hadn't been ushered out of there like a skunk in a perfume factory.

"But Bigelow, Timmy kicked me out. He doesn't want my help anymore."

"He does," Bigelow insisted. "He is just very afraid. Fear often makes us do foolish things. Before you can help Timmy defeat his monsters, you must first break the grip of fear."

"How do I do that?"

"Fear grips the body along with the mind, Will. And breaking fear's grip on the body can, in turn, help *free* the mind as well," Bigelow instructed. "The first step is to steady your breathing. Fear makes your heart race and your breathing become quick and shallow. If you focus on inhaling deeply, you can slow down and relax your breaths. Steadying your breathing will calm your body and help clear your mind. Then you can see past the fear and focus your thoughts on the task at hand."

"What..." I stuttered hesitantly. "What if that's not enough? What if I can't figure out what to do?"

"You can. When your mind is clear, you will know what must be done. But an important part of triumphing over monsters is overcoming such doubts."

"How?" I protested. "When I defeated my own monsters, you were there the whole time telling me what to do. How will I ever manage it without you?"

"You have already proven yourself, Will. But you must convince yourself that you are capable. No one else can do it for you. Talk to yourself. Remind yourself that you have triumphed before, and you shall do so again."

"But...but *can* I?" I whispered. "Can I really?"

"Without a doubt," Bigelow said firmly. "You will be brilliant. I have complete and utter confidence in you."

For a minute, my eyes wandered as I stood silently thinking over all Bigelow had told me.

"Well, okay. I'll give it another try," I finally said. Then I focused a weak smile on him. "Thanks for your help, Bigelow. I guess those are all the questions I have right now."

"No problem," he smiled in that toothy, monster way of his. "I'm always here if you need me. And just remember one more thing, Will: things are always less scary when you face them with a friend."

And with that, he pulled the blanket back over himself, climbed back onto the bed next to Teddy, and vanished.

Chapter Fourteen – Sticky Subjects

If the night before had been a lousy one, the morning that followed quickly started to look even worse. For starters, my mom made breakfast. Now, that may not sound so bad to *you*, but then you've never sampled my mother's cooking. Believe me, once you've tasted her notorious spinach and onion pancakes, you become a big fan of Tony the Tiger. After a short time spent stifling my gag reflex so that I could down a few bites, and a long time spent listening to my mom lecture me about the importance of a healthy diet, I dashed out the door, late for my bus.

Again.

The last few kids were still stepping up the stairs of the bus as I sprinted to the bus stop. I ran up and jumped through the doors just as the driver began closing them, which caused me to land awkwardly on the second step and spill my books onto the floor. The bus driver scowled down at me as I knelt to pick them up. Her breath smelled like she had just sampled my mom's garlic kale chowder.

"Thank you for joining us this morning," she said sharply. "Now find yourself a seat! I've got a schedule to keep!"

I quickly stood myself back up, and when I raised my eyes I noticed a dark-haired girl in a track uniform snickering at me from her seat in the second row. I managed an awkward smile, but just then...

"Will!" a very excited voice called out. The sound tugged at my ear and drew my gaze down the aisle to where Jeannine was waiting for me. She stood out from the rest of the kids on the bus like a neon sign, partially because she was wearing some glowing necklaces that made her *look* like a neon sign. She was sitting alone, dressed in one of her usual tie-dyed shirts and a black leather vest, in a seat seven rows down, right next to the emergency exit as always. When I started making my way toward her, she began bouncing up and down in her seat, and she pounced when I was still two rows away.

"So, how did it go last night?" she gushed eagerly. "Did you find the monster? Did you..."

"Excuse me," I interrupted gruffly. "I seem to remember us saying something about keeping our... *business*...a secret."

Jeannine gasped, and clasped her hand to her mouth.

"Oh, right," she mumbled through her fingers, which were covered with black nail polish and several gothic skull rings. She sat back down and looked around as if to check whether or not anyone was listening, then motioned for me to join her. I walked down the aisle, but a large shoebox was filling up most of the seat beside her.

"What's that?" I asked as Jeannine quickly picked up the box and sat it on her lap. I plopped down in the seat next to her, noticing as I did that she had added streaks of hot pink to her dyed black hair, which matched the pink paper clips she wore as earrings. That meant it must be Wednesday, because Wednesday is Jeannine's pink day.

"It's my diorama," she said excitedly. "Remember? The science project that's due today? Where's yours?"

Unfortunately, I had been so focused on monsters lately that I'd completely forgotten that our projects were due. It's funny how fighting for your life will do that to you.

"I...I forgot mine," I mumbled.

"Will Allen!" she said in her high and mighty tone of voice. "I think you'd forget your head if it weren't attached."

I don't know about you, but that tone always gets under my skin.

"Well, if I can just *keep* it attached," I grumbled irritably, "then I won't have anything to worry about, will I?"

"You're going to lose points if you turn it in late," she chided. "So now maybe someone else can win the outstanding science student award for a change."

"You're just jealous!" I retorted crossly. "Anyway, with all the stuff your mom signs you up for, what with the music lessons, acting lessons, gymnastics classes, skating lessons and all, I doubt you had time to come up with anything very good."

"For your information," she said loftily, turning her nose upward, "she's also got me a science tutor. And my tutor says that this is the best diorama she's ever seen."

I snickered, and rolled my eyes.

"Well, that's some compliment," I chuckled. "Kind of like saying the best camel poop I ever smelled."

Jeannine just gave a harrumph and pulled her diorama away from me, like the cardboard box had been offended.

We didn't talk the rest of the way to school. Without Jeannine's usual blabber to listen to, the ride seemed much longer, so I just sat there thinking about all of the things that might go wrong with my day. When we finally got to school though, everything went fine.

At least until Science Class.

Now just so you know, Science has always been my favorite subject. I suppose that's because I've always been fascinated with examining things and learning how they work (but don't tell my dad that – he's still upset about the time I took apart his TV and then tried to put in back together again). That class takes place just before lunch, which is a good thing, because if it was *after* lunch, Jeannine would probably throw up from the formaldehyde smell in the room, just like she did last year. We're talking major puke-o-rama.

"Mr. Allen," called out Mr. Munson, our science teacher. "Where is your science project?"

Now *I* was the one who felt like throwing up.

"I...ah, I forgot it, sir," I replied weakly.

"You forgot?" the teacher said, tilting his head and looking down his nose at me (and given the size of that nose, it was a long way down). "I've been reminding the class every day for two weeks!"

"Yes sir. I'm sorry sir," was all I could say.

"Very well," he answered as his glasses began riding down the slope of his nose. He pulled them off his face and cleaned the lenses on the lapel of his worn tweed jacket, then put them back on and announced, "Ten points will be taken from your project grade…"

"T- ten points?" I sputtered.

"And ten more for each additional day it is late," he continued.

"But…but sir! I'm up for the science award! Ten points could ruin my chances…"

"I know you are up for the award, Mr. Allen. I am the one who nominated you, remember?" Mr. Munson reminded. "But being up for the award does not excuse you from turning in assignments on time. Quite the contrary, it adds the responsibility of setting a good example for the rest of the class! Now, I will expect to see your project on my desk tomorrow. No excuses!"

"I don't believe...!" I started barking, but then I melted under the power of Mr. Munson's firm stare. "...Um, that is...yes sir."

Behind me, the sound of muffled snickering arose. When Mr. Munson turned and began writing on the board, I shot a quick glance back. In the last row of seats, two large piles of wasted space sat huddled together, giggling stupidly. One boy was long and stringy, wearing jeans, a leather jacket, loafers, and a sickening sneer beneath the huge wave of golden hair covering his face. The other was as engorged as an elephant, wearing a football jacket, cut-off sweats, and a bleached blond buzz-cut above his huge flat face.

"Oooouuuuw! The teacher's pet got told!" the elephant-sized boy snorted, jabbing his finger in my direction as though someone might not know who he was talking about.

"Not so smart now, are you, bright boy?" the other boy hissed. Then he crumpled up a piece of paper from his notebook and threw it at me. I batted it away deftly, but that only seemed to signal to the bigger one that this was a new game to play.

"Hey, let me try!"

So then the two of them took turns chucking balls of rolled up paper at my head. Now, these goons were exactly the kind of guys that can be experts at making life at school miserable. The old Will Allen might have squeamishly turned away, but Monster Detective Will Allen wasn't going to stand for it.

"Knock it off!" I whispered fiercely. I picked up some of the paper balls from where they landed on the floor and chucked them back at those jerks.

"Oooouuuw!" the big one said gleefully. "Little Jimmy Neutron bites back!"

"That is *not* my name..."

"Ahem." The voice came from right above me. I spun in my seat and looked up, and there was Mr. Munson. His arms were folded tightly, and frown lines radiated out from his furrowed brow.

"Have you dropped something, Mr. Allen?"

"Um, no sir," I said weakly, crumpling the wad of paper in my hand tightly and turning back to face the board.

"Good. Then I should not find any pieces of paper on the ground after class, should I? Of course, if any bits of debris – say, some crumpled up balls of paper – do find their way to the floor, I expect that you will pick them up before you leave."

The snickering behind me rose once more. Mr. Munson lifted his eyes and fixed them on the pair of troublemakers in the back of the room. Instantly, they straightened and quieted themselves. The teacher then turned his gaze from them back to me, nodded knowingly, and then retreated to the board.

"Now, regarding the table on page forty-seven, there seems to have been some confusion..."

As soon as Mr. Munson turned his back, whispering started up behind me again. I sat quietly, fuming with anger and frustration. I mean, I was proud of myself for having stood up to the twin lunkheads that had been pestering me, but at that moment I realized that, unlike the monsters in my room, confronting horrible creatures at school was not an automatic ticket to a brighter day.

Chapter Fifteen – Unwelcome Requests

When I finally got to lunch, I was too bummed to eat.
I sat poking at my macaroni & cheese, which looked
suspiciously like one of the creatures that had lurked in
the corner of my room the night Bigelow and I battled
my monsters.   Just to be safe, I pulled out my
MonsterScope to check it out.

"So, are you going to eat that?" I heard Jeannine
giggle from behind me. "Or is it going to eat *you*?"

I turned to look at her, checking her out with the
MonsterScope as well.

Hey, you never know.

"Have you come to gloat?" I asked sharply.

"Don't be such a sourpuss. It's not the end of the world."

"Ten points! My grade could end up being...*average*!"

"Oh, come on, Will," she said as she plopped down
next to me. "Lighten up! You'll still win your precious
science award. You always do."

I shrugged, and looked away.

"Oh, come on!" she insisted, and stomped me on the foot. I hate when she does that, especially since she always wears steel-toed construction boots.

"Oooww! All right already!" I moaned.

Jeannine glared at me, but I glowered right back.

"Anyway," she continued casually, turning her gaze to the table, "If you really want to get depressed, just check this out."

Jeannine opened her lunch bag and took out several zipper-sealed plastic bags.

"Alfalfa sprouts, green bean stew, carrot juice, and for dessert..."

"Sweet potato mousse," I grumbled without turning to look. "Give your mom credit...at least she's consistent."

And then we both stopped talking. Jeannine just kept staring at me like she was expecting something.

"Well, are you going to tell me or what?" she finally blurted.

"Tell you what?" I growled back.

"What happened at Timmy's house last night?" Jeannine said impatiently. "Did you find the monster? Did you take care of it?"

I didn't say anything. I don't know if it was because I didn't want to tell her or because I simply didn't know what to say, but instead of answering I began fumbling awkwardly with the latches on my lunchbox.

"Will," Jeannine said in a suddenly serious voice, "Did...did something go wrong? Did something bad happen?"

"No," I answered. "*Nothing* happened. That's the problem. And Timmy..."

Just as I spoke his name, Timmy appeared right in front of me. It kind of spooked me out at first. He just stood in my face and growled.

"Stop bothering me!" he shouted.

Naturally, I had no idea what he was talking about.

"Um, define bothering," I suggested.

"I mean it!" he went on. "If you don't stop it I'll..."

"Stop what?" I yelled back heatedly. "I'm not doing anything."

"Stop it with the business cards! It's driving me crazy! They turn up everywhere now: in my backpack, in my pocket, on my pillow. There was even one in my breakfast cereal this morning!"

Jeannine snorted, and milk came up through her nose. That made us both start laughing.

"Stop it!" Timmy yelled. "It's not funny!"

"Oh, I'm *so* sorry," I said scornfully. "But since you don't want my help anymore, there's not much I..."

"Doesn't want your help?" Jeannine injected. "Timmy doesn't want you to help get rid of his..."

She looked around to be sure no one was listening.

"...his *you know what*?" she finished, turning back to Timmy and fixing him with an intent stare. "Is that true?"

When Jeannine looked at him, Timmy's whole manner changed. He softened, looked down, and kicked at the floor.

"Yes, well...I...uh..."

"Timmy," Jeannine said softly, batting her eyelashes, "Didn't you ask me the other day to help you with your English homework? Do you want me to come tutor you?"

"Really?" Timmy said, his eyes suddenly wide. "Yeah! Can you come over this afternoon? I've got a big essay exam coming up..."

"Well, I would," she said slyly. "But I think it might be a bit too dangerous to come to a house that has a monster running loose."

Timmy's face sank, and he deflated like a balloon.

"Oh, right," he said as his body drooped.

"But maybe," Jeannine offered, "maybe if you and Will can work together to get rid of the monster, then it would be safe for me to come over."

"I, um...yeah. I guess that would be a good idea..."

Timmy's expression grew twitchy and confused, like his brain was processing more thoughts than it could handle, which it probably was. He finally turned back to me and kind of mumbled, "Can you come over tonight, Will?"

Jeannine turned to me and smiled. I gave her a quick smirk back before I turned to Timmy and said, "I can't

110

tonight. I have to finish my science project. Make it tomorrow instead."

"Okay then, tomorrow," Timmy replied. He then looked back at Jeannine and waved.

"Bye then," he said.

"Bye, Timmy," she answered as he backed away smiling stupidly and tripping over a mop and bucket. Jeannine just giggled.

"Well, I guess you're back on the case," she said.

"But I'm not sure I want to *be* back on the case," I protested.

Jeannine coughed one of those *I forgot how to breathe* coughs.

"What?" she stammered. "Why not? Yesterday you were *thrilled* about becoming a monster detective."

Once again, I could come up with nothing to say, so I turned and looked away.

"What's wrong, Will?" she asked urgently. "*Really.* You said I'd be your partner, remember? You have to tell me what's going on."

I slowly exhaled, and then looked back at her.

"Jeannine, did you ever get the feeling," I asked, "that everything is getting out of control?"

Jeannine's eyes lit up for a second, but then she put her hands together and frowned.

"Will," she said pointedly. "My mother tries to plan out my every waking moment. When do I ever even imagine things are *in* my control?"

She tried not to let it show, but her face twitched a bit, like she was caught between feeling sad and angry.

111

"Sorry," I finally said. "I'm really sorry. All *my* mom does is ground me if I come home after 8:00."

"Don't worry about it," she said casually. "Now tell me what's wrong."

"I..." I began. "It's just that this monster detective stuff isn't like I thought it'd be. Last night, Timmy threw me out and told me I was useless..."

"Oh, don't let him get to you," Jeannine injected. "He's just..."

I cut her off.

"He was *right*," I told her. "I can't get rid of monsters; I can only try to shine light on them! Timmy's the one who has to face them down. And it doesn't exactly seem like he's eager to do that."

"Well, I don't know. Maybe now that he has the right incentive, he will be," Jeannine said. I didn't share her optimism.

"This bites!" I griped. "What good is it being a monster detective with no monster fighting powers of my own? That's like Spiderman without his webs, or Superman without his x-ray vision, or Plastic Man without his...well, his plastic."

"Actually, you're more like a Batman who's a bit too batty," Jeannine retorted. I glared at her.

"You are *so* not helping," I snarled.

"Well then, *let* me help," she proposed, slapping her hands down. "Why don't you give me a crack at this?"

"What? What do you mean?" I sputtered.

"Let me help with the case," she suggested. "Tell me what's gone wrong."

I thought it over, and decided, *Well, why not?*

"Okay, look," I said. "Let me make this simple. To defeat monsters, we need light and bravery. *My* light, as it turns out, but *Timmy's* bravery. The problem is, I have the bravery, but Timmy has the light."

Jeannine scratched her head. Whenever she does that, I pretty much know what she's going to say next.

"I don't get it," she finally blurted.

"Bigelow gave me a special flashlight. He calls it a RevealeR. The light it shines lets you see the hidden truth about your monsters," I explained. "Timmy has to see his monsters for what they really are, and face them. But he won't do it."

"Can't you do it for him?"

"No. I can only shine the light. But I *have* no light."

"Why not?"

"Bigelow said that I need to understand the truth about the monsters before I can get the flashlight to work. You see, the RevealeR, it...it turns truth into light. That's what I have to use to fight the monsters."

"Can't you get rid of monsters without the flashlight?"

"No," I moaned. "I need the RevealeR to show Timmy the truth about the monsters and make them shrink. Without the RevealeR, we have no weapon to fight the monsters once we've found them. There's no other way to make the light."

Jeannine took a deep breath and pursed her lips, then scratched her head some more.

"You could always try rubbing two sticks together," she suggested.

I scowled at her.

"This is *not* helping!" I barked. "The point is: I've got to figure out what that monster really is before I become its late-night snack."

Jeannine didn't have an answer for that, so we sat there quietly a while.

"So then," she finally said. "We need to come up with a plan.

"A plan?"

"Yes, a plan! If you want to solve this properly, you've got to have a plan for what you're going to do."

"A plan, huh? Okay, how's this for a plan?" I posed. "When I get to his house tomorrow, I'm going to grill Timmy. If I force him to tell me more about the monster, then maybe I can learn what happened that caused it to come into our world. Once I discover the source of the monster, it should be simple enough to figure out why it's here and what it wants. Then I can use my flashlight to show Timmy the truth about it so that he can face it, and it'll shrink like it's supposed to."

I smiled, certain that I had just come up with an infallible plan. But Jeannine scowled at me.

"And how exactly," she asked, "are you going to *force* him to tell you anything?"

My smile crumbled like my mother's peanut butter and flax seed cookies {don't ask}.

"Um, I don't know," I said.

"Well, if you're going to try figure out how to get information out of Timmy," Jeannine suggested, "maybe two heads would be better than one. Why don't I come along?"

I looked at her like she had just grown horns.

"Jeannine," I said crossly. "*I'm* the detective, remember? You've never even *seen* a monster. You wouldn't know what to do."

"Neither did you, until Bigelow showed you," she reminded. "And in case you hadn't noticed, *I* was the one who convinced Timmy to let you get back on the case. You may be good with monsters, Will, but I'm a lot better at dealing with people."

"But...but Jeannine," I protested. "You're a..."

A *Girl*. But I guessed that if I said that, she might get snippy.

"Um, that is, aren't you...you know..."

Afraid? Another sure kettle-boiler.

"Ah, let me think it over," I finally concluded.

Chapter Sixteen - Dodges

I had trouble focusing on my homework that night, and my science project, a giant model of how lasers work, was still dripping from the sloppy gobs of glue I had used to put it together when the phone rang.

"Have you thought it over, Will?" Jeannine asked without so much as a hello.

"Not now, Jeannine," I answered. "I'm trying to concentrate on my schoolwork."

"Concentrate on your schoolwork?" Jeannine scoffed. "*Really*? Then why do I hear the sound of your TV in the background?"

"That's not *my* TV," I told her. "The sound is coming in through my window. The neighbors always have the volume up too high. It's actually really annoying."

"Harrumph!" she replied. "Just promise me that you will think about it?"

"I promise," I said. "Now would you mind letting me get back to work?"

"Okay. Bye," she said, and hung up. I slammed down the receiver.

Well actually, I didn't really slam it, because I already broke one phone last year and I didn't think my parents would believe me this time if I told them that one of the monsters did it. But I definitely felt like slamming something. The truth was that I *had* been thinking about it, and there was no way I saw anything good coming from Jeannine being in that room with me, Timmy, and the monsters. How could I protect her from being eaten alive, when I wasn't even sure I could protect *myself?*

Of course, she couldn't let it go.

"So, have you thought it over, Will?" was how she greeted me on the school bus the following morning.

"Have you thought it over, Will?" quickly became the phrase of the day. I heard it in class, at lunch, and on the bus ride home. Ten minutes after I came in the door, the phone rang.

"Have you thought it over, Will?" Jeannine said.

I hung up the phone. For the rest of the afternoon, every time my mother called out to me to say I had a phone call, which was about every five minutes, I told her I had to go to the bathroom.

Finally, evening came, and I prepared to set out for Timmy's house. Then the phone rang one more time.

"Will," my mother called out. "It's for you. Jeannine is on the phone. Would you please take it this time?"

"Sorry, mom," I said, quickly throwing on my coat and hat. "I've got to run over to Timmy's house. Tell her I'll call her back."

"Do you think you can make it all the way there without stopping?" my mother said tartly. "Or should I send you with a port-a-potty?"

"I think I can hold it," I said dryly as I headed for the door.

My mother shook her head as I marched out.

"I hope they have a lot of toilet tissue in that house," she muttered as she turned away.

"Well," Timmy's mom said as she let me in. "With all this tutoring, I certainly expect to see a big improvement in Timmy's math grade this term."

"Uh, right," I answered, thinking as I did that I wanted to be nowhere near this house when the next report card showed up. But then, I would have to survive a battle with terrifying monsters before worrying about that.

That's one of the great things about this job: it helps put everything else in perspective.

Timmy came into the foyer from his kitchen. He quickly hid something behind his back when his mother spotted him.

"Oh, hi Will," he said nervously. "Well, come on, we've got a lot of work to do." And then he grabbed my arm again and began tugging.

"Just a minute, young man," his mother stopped him. "What's that behind your back?"

Timmy tried to turn away from her, but his mom reached around behind his back and pulled from his hand a bunch of chocolate bars.

"Sneaking food up to your room again?" she scolded. "How many times have I told you..."

"It's for Will," Timmy said. "He told me that I should make sure I had lots of chocolate for him to snack on when he's...ah, tutoring."

Timmy's mother glared at me accusingly.

"Oh, really?" she scoffed.

"I, ah...It helps me think," I offered. She obviously wasn't buying it, because the scowl lines began growing deep on her face again.

"You're here to study, not have a party," she said sternly. Then she took the bars and ushered us out of the foyer to the stairs.

"Oh, and Timmy, you left the phone off the hook. *Again*! You need to start behaving more responsibly, young man."

"Right, mom," Timmy said mechanically. "Sorry, mom." He said no more, but when we got to the top of the stairs, he turned to me and smiled as he pulled several more chocolate bars out of his pockets.

"I'm *way* ahead of her," he said smugly.

When Timmy opened the door to his room, I couldn't believe my eyes.

"What happened here? Did a monster do this?" I asked, staring at the frenzied mess the room had become. Clothes, books, toys, and furniture were strewn everywhere. On the far side of the room, the mattress was off the bed and propped up horizontally, with stacks of books piled around the sides to form a makeshift bunker. Inside the bunker were a net, baseballs, a bat, a hockey stick, and a football helmet. Lying on the floor in the center of the room was an empty plate, and standing next to it was the Timmy's end table, but the phone that had been on top of it, the one I'd spotted monster trails on, was nowhere in sight. Timmy walked to the middle of the room and placed the chocolate bars down on the plate.

"It's the bait," Timmy explained. "I hope this one works."

"You're trying to trap it?" I asked.

Timmy nodded.

"I tried yesterday, too," he explained. "I told my mom I needed an extra peanut butter and jelly sandwich for lunch, but she gave me liverwurst! Even monsters won't eat liverwurst!"

"Timmy," I said exasperatedly. "It won't work. I know from experience, it won't work."

"You've tried trapping monsters?" he asked.

I nodded. "With a brownie ice cream sundae," I told him.

"And it *didn't work*?" He seemed shocked.

"No," I said flatly. "Monsters don't eat regular food. They feed off of our fears. And I'm sure you've been giving them a steady diet of that."

"Well, why didn't you tell me that in the first place?" Timmy asked crossly.

Because I didn't know, I thought. But I wasn't telling Timmy that.

"Well, maybe this time you'll keep me around long enough to tell you what you need to know." I answered instead. Timmy gave me a sheepish look.

"Look, I'm sorry about... about kicking you out the other night..."

"Never mind!" I said irritably. "Let's just clear some room in this mess so that I can get to work. With my luck, I'll trip over one of these toys in the dark and break my neck."

I didn't say, *before the monsters have a chance to do it for me.* But I was thinking it.

There was barely enough room to take another step, so I got down and began sweeping the toys and books into piles at the side of the room. I looked back, expecting to see Timmy doing the same, but he was in his bunker, putting on the football helmet.

"What are you doing?" I asked angrily.

"Putting on protection," he answered. "You never know when a monster might try to pierce your skull and suck out your brains."

"Oh, you don't know what you're talking about," I grumbled. But I secretly began wishing that I had brought a helmet too.

"All right," I announced. "That's good enough. Let's get started."

I walked over to the light switch on the wall.

"Are you ready?" I asked as I held my hand to the switch. Timmy, crouching in his bunker with his helmet drooping in front of his eyes and a hockey stick held tightly with both hands, nodded. I flicked the switch. The room went dark, and that eerie blue glow that had filled it two nights before returned. I held my breath, then flicked the switch on my flashlight. It flickered a bit, and sputtered like an old man gagging on dry toast (or more likely, on my mother's oat bran and wheat germ waffles), but then a very dim trickle of fizzy greenish light came pouring out.

"It looks like you need new batteries," Timmy said.

"It doesn't take batteries," I answered. "It's...uh, rechargeable."

"And you didn't charge it before coming?" Timmy complained.

"It's charged!" I insisted. "It just needs a little time to warm up."

"Well it better warm up fast!" Timmy said urgently. His hands were starting to shake. "It won't be long before..."

All of a sudden, there was a knocking sound. It started softly, but then grew louder, echoing throughout the room. I swung my flashlight around in every direction to try and spot where it was coming from.

"It's here!" Timmy bellowed. "It's here! Turn on the light! See if it ate the chocolate!"

"I told you, it doesn't want chocolate! Now be quiet!" I ordered.

The knocking sound continued, but my light still wasn't spying anything. Something was very wrong.

Just then, the door to the room began shaking violently. Timmy hid behind me while I turned the beam of my RevealeR to the door and shined my light on it, but it revealed nothing at all. Then the shaking stopped, and we both breathed a small sigh of relief.

Suddenly, there was a loud bang, and the door shook once more. Timmy fell back and whimpered. The room turned quiet as death, but then there was another loud bang, and the door exploded open.

Chapter Seventeen - Collaborations

Into the doorway stepped a dark silhouette. Its shape was very much like that of a pterodactyl.

"Stupid door!" the figure in the shadows muttered. "...Should have had that fixed ages ago..."

"Look out!" Timmy cried out. "It's the monster!"

"Relax," I said, lowering my flashlight. "It's just your mom."

"Same thing," Timmy muttered.

"What's going on in here?" Timmy's mother called to us as she pushed her way into the room. "How can you study math in a pitch-black room?"

Timmy and I exchanged one of those *'I don't have an answer for that, do you?'* kind of looks.

"Um, we were taking a break," I stuttered quickly, hiding my flashlight in my back pocket while Timmy kicked the plate of chocolate bars under his bed. "There were some fireflies outside, and we turned out the light so we could..."

"What are you doing, checking up on me?" Timmy spouted angrily.

"No," his mother said firmly. "I've been knocking on your door to tell you that you have another guest."

"Another guest?" Timmy spat. "Who?"

And from behind Timmy's mother, another dark silhouette stepped into the doorway. It was a smaller, thinner figure in a daisy-covered dress, who walked into the light with a haughty stiffness in her step.

"*Jeannine*?" I sputtered. "I thought I told you…"

"I thought it over about you thinking it over," she said firmly. "And then I decided that I was done thinking about whether I should let you go on thinking about it. So, here I am."

After unraveling what she had just said, I wasn't quite sure whether I admired her gumption or hated it. But one thing I *was* sure of was that there wasn't much I could do about it either way.

"What's with the dress?" I grumbled with a sour look on my face. "Since when do you wear…*flowery* stuff?"

Jeannine just smirked and glanced over at Timmy, but before she could speak…

"What's in heaven's name have you been doing in here?" Timmy's mother spouted as she looked around the room. The sight of that terrible mess seemed to horrify her more than any giant flying shark ever could. "Have you two been fighting?"

"No!" Timmy answered crossly.

"Then why is everything strewn all over the room like this? And why in the world are you wearing your father's old football helmet?"

She reached over and pulled the helmet off of his head.

"Honestly!" she grumbled. "I don't see how you could need this to study math!"

"Ooowww! But mom," Timmy protested. "I need to protect myself from the...you know..."

"Enough of this nonsense!" his mother declared. "I want this room cleaned up immediately, young man!"

Timmy's head slumped, but then he caught sight of Jeannine. She was pointedly looking away from him with an embarrassed expression on her face. Timmy's posture suddenly stiffened.

"It's *my* room!" Timmy challenged defiantly. "If I don't mind the mess, neither should you!"

His mother gave Timmy a withering look.

"You'll clean this room right now or I'll give you something to *really* be scared of!" she declared, and then she stormed out of the room and slammed the door. Jeannine and I stood gaping at the door, totally speechless.

"Still think she's not a monster?" Timmy asked.

"Well," Jeannine responded. "I'd certainly be terrified if that was hiding under *my* bed."

"Well, there's nothing I can do," I added glumly. "I'm a monster detective, not a social worker. Come on, let's get back to work."

"Okay, let's," Jeannine agreed. Timmy and I stared at her.

"Jeannine..." I said.

"I'm a part of the team," she said with her *and that's final* tone of voice. "I'm staying."

"Jeannine," I said. "You can't. You don't have any of the...*detective* stuff you need."

"Like what?" she asked huffily.

"Well, for one thing, you would need a..." I began saying, but then a strange thing happened. When I reached into my back pocket to take out my special flashlight, I found *two* there. The first was my RevealeR, the faded red one that Bigelow had given me, but there was another one that was yellow and decorated all over with little pink daisies. Naturally, I handed Jeannine the yellow one.

"I think this must be for you," I said.

You'd think that she'd be thrilled to have her own RevealeR, but she looked at it suspiciously.

"Yours is bigger," she complained.

In case I forgot to mention it yet, Jeannine can sometimes be a real pain in the... you know what.

"Bigelow said size doesn't matter," I barked.

"Fine," she answered. "Then you won't mind if I get the bigger one."

"This one is *mine*," I hissed. "It's the one Bigelow gave me. This new one is obviously for a girl, I mean, just look at it. It has *daisies*!"

Jeannine didn't answer, she just stomped on my foot. I growled at her, but just then Timmy spoke up.

"Excuse me, but who is Bigelow?"

"Never mind," I answered grumpily.

"I still need a magnifying glass," Jeannine pointed out.

"A MonsterScope," I corrected.

"Whatever!" Jeannine growled. "The point is, I need one!"

I reached into my other pocket for my MonsterScope, but there was still just one. I held it up.

"Just one," I showed her. "Sorry."

"Well then, what do I use?" she complained.

"I don't know. Maybe you can try using your glasses."

Did I mention before that Jeannine wears glasses? I guess it never came up. She usually only wears them for reading because she thinks they make her look dorky. Anyway, she took them out of her pocket, studied them a bit, and then put them on, squinting strangely. She *did* look dorky.

"But, how do I turn them on?" she asked.

"Hey!" Timmy called out. "What about me? Don't I get some kind of monster-fighting ray gun or something?"

128

Jeannine and I just turned and stared at him, Jeannine with that weird squinty look, and me with my magnifying glass in front of my eye like a giant monocle.

"Just leave this to the professionals," I told him.

"Harrumph!" Timmy growled irritably. He pulled the plate of chocolate out from under the bed, put it back in the center of the room, and then he climbed over one of the stacks of books and sat behind the propped up mattress.

"Wait a minute," I said. "Where are you going?"

"Into my fort, where it's safe," he answered.

I glared at him, and asked pointedly, "Then how do you expect to find the monsters?"

"You're the detective," he spat. "*Detect* something!"

I looked back at Jeannine, but she just shrugged.

"Fine!" I said impatiently. "We'll try it *your* way. Let's get started then."

And I walked over and turned out the light, then Jeannine and I joined Timmy behind his makeshift barricades.

An hour later, we were still sitting there, bored, and growing restless.

"There!" Timmy cried out. "Something is moving over there! Is that it?"

I lifted my MonsterScope looked through the glass at where he pointed. What looked like waves of creepy black fingers were crawling across the floor, drifting back and forth in time with the blowing winds outside. But there were no glowing tracks or prints anywhere.

"No," I said plainly. "Those are just shadows from the tree outside."

"What about that over there?" he swiftly added. "Those clumps under my desk. Are those, like... monster droppings or something?"

I bent down and checked it out with the MonsterScope.

"No, those are just dust bunnies," I said dejectedly.

"This is boring," Jeannine complained.

"You wanted to be a detective," I pointed out. "This is what it's like."

"But can't we *do* something?" she whined.

"Not while we're hiding back here, no."

Timmy scowled.

"What's wrong with these stupid monsters?" he complained. "Why won't they eat this stuff?"

"I told you before," I groused. I was feeling rather ornery at this point. "This isn't what they want. The only bait that will work is *you*."

"Thanks *so* much," Timmy replied. "But it's not my goal in life to be a monster's happy meal!"

"More like an *un*happy meal," Jeannine grumbled.

"What?" he turned to her. "What's that?"

"Never mind!" I snapped. "You know, I'm not interested in being monster chow either! But I'm here!" Then I turned and pointed at Jeannine.

"We *both* came here to help you! Both of us are here to fight monsters for you! But we have to do this my way. Now are you ready to face this monster or not?"

Timmy looked at me, and then over a Jeannine, who stood firm. Then he looked down.

"Even a *girl*," he mumbled, "Even a girl is braver than me."

Timmy squirmed and kicked at the ground, but wouldn't look up at us. He seemed to be ashamed that Jeannine was prepared to face the danger that he shied away from.

*Okay, maybe something good **can** come from having her around*, I thought.

"All right," Timmy finally said. "What should I do?"

"For a start," I instructed, "let's all come out of hiding."

I stepped out from behind the barricades and walked to the center of the room. As I turned and looked back, Jeannine stood and climbed over a pile of books and joined me. Timmy hesitated, scanning the room nervously, but when nothing jumped out at us he breathed a heavy sigh, held his breath, and strode gingerly out of his place of safety and into the eerie darkness that spread before us.

Chapter Eighteen - Courtesies

Timmy kept glancing around nervously, twitching his head to the sound of every rustle of the leaves or chirping of crickets that drifted in through the stillness all around us. With every shudder and tremble that ran up Timmy's spine, the shadows around us seemed to grow deeper and darker.

"Well, now what?" Timmy blurted.

"Don't worry," I told him. "I have a plan."

I picked up the plate of chocolate bars and put them on the desk.

"Now," I said firmly, "we set our trap with the only thing that works: live bait." Then I pulled a chair into the center of the room.

"Sit down," I instructed.

"Don't mind if I do," Jeannine said casually as she took off her glasses and slid them into her pocket, then plopped down into the chair. "That floor was very uncomfortable..."

"Not you!" I growled. "Timmy! Timmy has to sit there!"

"Oh, right," she said sheepishly, jumping up at once.

"But...but my dad says it's not polite for a gentleman to take a lady's seat..." Timmy protested.

"Down!" I ordered.

"Humph! Some people have no manners," Timmy grumbled as he sat himself in the chair. His eyes immediately began darting around anxiously, and the room grew darker still. I flicked the switch on my flashlight, which hummed to life, but still with only that very dim, greenish light.

"I told you that you should have charged that thing!" Timmy said nervously.

"Oh, shut up!" I barked. "Now stop whining and tell us what it is you're so scared of."

"I'm scared of the monsters, you idiot!" Timmy shouted. "What else would I be…"

Just then, a loud ringing began echoing all through the room. Timmy froze like a stone, but I immediately pointed my RevealeR and attempted to trace the noise to its source. The sound led me across the room to Timmy's desk, which was littered with books, papers, pens, ink cartridges…you name it. I dug through a pile of papers and found Timmy's phone underneath.

"Yes!" I cheered. "I've found the…wait…"

I checked out the phone with my MonsterScope, but there were no glowing spots on it this time. And there was no ring there either. It was just a plain old telephone.

"But…but that can't be…" I muttered. "Something was there last time. I know it was!"

So I looked closer, searching for any signs of a monster, but nothing appeared in the sight of my scope. But as I leaned in further, I noticed something. Something important.

The receiver was slightly ajar. The phone had been left off the hook.

*Timmy, you left the phone off the hook. **Again.*** His mother had said that. Timmy must have been leaving the phone off the hook a lot. I looked over at him as he sat in the center of the room, and saw him staring nervously back.

"I wonder…" I muttered softly, and then I lifted the receiver and placed it properly on the base of the phone. Timmy's eyes grew wide, and his teeth began chattering.

"S-stop…stop messing with my stuff!" he sputtered.

Without a word, I put the receiver back the way it was. Instantly, Timmy's eyes relaxed and he exhaled deeply. But then the ringing continued, and he stiffened again.

"He...he's been doing it on *purpose*," I whispered to myself.

As that thought filled my brain, the beam of light from my flashlight brightened with gleaming sparkles, though overall it still remained rather dim.

"Timmy," I asked, "who have you been getting phone calls from?"

"No one!" he screeched. "I don't know what you're talking about!"

"Then why are you so afraid of the phone ringing?"

"I'm not! I...I..."

But just as suddenly as it began, the ringing stopped. I shined my flashlight all around, but still saw no signs of the monster. Timmy sighed with relief, but then...

"I'm...sorry..." spoke a loud, high-pitched, echoing voice. "I'm...sorry...but..."

"NO!" Timmy cried out. "No! Go away!"

And he jumped out of the chair and dashed back to his fortress, but he tripped over one of the books in the dark and went sprawling. He knocked over one of the piles of books and crashed into his dresser, knocking down a heavy bookend that crashed to the floor inches from his head.

"I'm...sorry," the voice followed him. "I'm... sorry, but...he can't..."

"No!" Timmy screamed from the floor as he crawled behind the mattress. "Leave me alone!"

"I'm sorry, but he can't...come...to the phone."

"Nooooooo!" Timmy cried.

"What is it?" I asked. "What voice is that?"

"Never mind what it is!" he shouted. "Just wave your wand or something and get rid of it!"

"It doesn't work that way," I told him. "You have to do what I tell you."

"I tried doing what you told me!" Timmy shouted. "And it nearly killed me!"

"You big baby!" I yelled. "You're not helping!"

"Neither are *you*," I was told. I froze, and shook my head in surprise, because the scolding hadn't come from Timmy. It was Jeannine.

"What? What are you saying?" I asked her angrily.

"I'm saying that you have the people skills of a gnat," she retorted.

"Well, don't sugar-coat it, Jeannine. Say what you really think!"

"I'm saying you could use a little tact," she said pointedly.

"And some manners!" Timmy added.

My entire face grew red hot as my eyes shot from one to the other.

"I don't need this!" I shouted.

"Yes you do," Jeannine insisted. "Have you gotten Timmy to tell you what we need to know?"

I glanced down at my flashlight. It was still dim.

"No," I answered.

"Then let *me* try."

I glowered at Jeannine, but then looked at Timmy, cowering behind his mattress, and decided to give in.

Yes, I really do hate doing that.

"All right," I mumbled grudgingly. I put my RevealeR back in my pocket and stepped aside. Jeannine walked over to Timmy, who was crouched and shivering. She knelt and put her hand on his shoulder.

"I'm sorry, but he... can't... come... to the phone," the monster voice called out.

Timmy and Jeannine shuddered together, and I wondered why the voice affected both of them like that, but not me.

"Timmy," Jeannine said softly. "I understand. You don't have to explain. I feel it too."

"You do?" I sputtered. "Well then..."

"Be quiet, Will!" she ordered, and then turned back to Timmy, who looked up at her timidly.

"Don't be mad at Will," she told him. "It's not the same for him. He doesn't know what it's like."

"What are you talking about?" I growled indignantly.

"Shut up, Will!" they said together. My body shook angrily, but finally I stiffened, and folded my arms.

"Fine!" I grumbled, and began drumming my fingers.

"Timmy," Jeannine said softly. "I know now what the monster is. But *where* is it, Timmy? I need for you to tell me where to find it."

Timmy shook and shivered, as if trying to shake off the words Jeannine spoke, but she gently stroked his arm, and he finally looked at up her and melted.

"Over there," he stuttered, pointing with a shaking finger. "It's in the top left drawer of my desk."

Jeannine smiled softly, and patted his shoulder. Then she got up and walked to the desk.

I was so flabbergasted that I just stood making some sloppy sputtering sounds as she stepped right past me.

"You *knew*?" I bellowed at Timmy. "You knew all along where it was?!"

But Timmy said nothing: he was staring fixedly at Jeannine as she approached the desk. She hesitated briefly in front of it, but then took hold of the handle and opened the drawer in one swift motion. A bright golden glow erupted from within.

"I'm sorry, but he... can't... come... to the phone," cried out the voice of the monster, louder than ever before. The drawer shook violently as the monster-voice erupted, but then was still.

"Jeannine!" I called out excitedly as I stepped up to examine the drawer with my MonsterScope. Floating within it, burning with power and malice, was the ring.

"Jeannine, you did it! You uncovered the monster! Good work!"

But Jeannine didn't seem too pleased with her success.

"I..." she stuttered, stumbling back from the desk. "I...have to go to the bathroom."

"Not now, Jeannine!" I said, but she grabbed my shirt and tugged hard.

"I really have to go..." she insisted.

Jeannine dragged me back from the drawer, and I focused hard on her face. Utter terror filled her eyes.

"Jeannine, it's just a little ring..." I protested.

"I have to go *now*!" she screeched, and then turned and ran for the door.

"You're running away? From a little ring?"

But Jeannine didn't stop. She reached the door and opened it, yet the room remained shrouded in blackness.

"You...you..." I sputtered. "You're such a *girl*!"

But Jeannine ran out and the door closed behind her, leaving me and Timmy alone and defenseless with the monster she had released.

Chapter Nineteen - Misgivings

I was still staring at the door in frozen disbelief when Timmy grabbed my sleeve and tugged hard.

"Why did you do that?" Timmy yelled. "You scared her away!"

I couldn't believe what I was hearing.

"*I* scared her?" I yelled back. "It wasn't me; it was this stupid little…"

I stopped yelling, because when I turned back to the desk, the golden ring was hovering in mid-air just inside the open drawer. Its eerie kaleidoscopic glow appeared strong and bright now even without using the MonsterScope. As I watched, it rose from the drawer and drifted toward us, slowly rotating like a planet in space. The center of the ring shimmered like a disco ball, and beams of light projected from it in every direction. The rays struck the walls, creating a sea of hazy blotches that danced around the room. As they moved, trails of very soft, distant whispers followed. I studied the images projected onto the wall, but they were just blurs of light and darkness. At least, that's what they were to *me*.

"Noooo!" Timmy cried. "Look what you've done! Keep that horrible thing away! Don't let it get me!"

"Keep *what* away?" I asked. "It's just..."

But again I stopped short. As I spun around, I caught sight of one of the blurs on the wall, and saw that it was *growing*. The blur pulsed and throbbed as it drifted across the wall, becoming larger and brighter. It kept growing until it was an oblong blob about as tall as Timmy and twice as wide. The pulsing continued, and then the blob began to swell like an inflating balloon. As we stared, speechless, the blob began thrusting in our direction, and finally pulled itself *right off the wall*. It kept coming toward us, growing ever larger. Gleaming tentacles sprouted from its sides as it approached.

"Is...is that...the monster?" Timmy asked.

"Well, it's definitely no dust bunny," I retorted.

Timmy began shivering. "Wha-what do we do *now*?"

"Face it!" I commanded. "If you ever hope to defeat this thing, then you've got to stand up to it!"

"Are you crazy!? Those glowing tentacles probably paralyze you with just a touch!"

"Good!" I shouted. "It can start with your mouth!"

Then I shoved him toward the monster. Timmy stumbled forward, then stiffened. When he finally looked up at the creature before him, he gasped for breath, but his lungs squealed like a rusty wheel when he tried to inhale. As the monster drew in close and rose high above him, Timmy cowered helplessly.

"I – I can't do this," he whimpered. "*Help me!*"

"Well, so much for *that* plan," I said quietly, steeling myself as I pulled my flashlight back out of my pocket, "I guess it's time to be a hero." Then I lifted my RevealeR and flicked the switch.

"Come on," I growled nervously. "I need some light...*now*!" But the RevealeR coughed and gurgled, and the light that erupted from it was still weak and feeble. I looked back at Timmy, and the glowing blob had begun to envelop him. Its tentacles wrapped themselves around him as if they were about to swallow him whole.

What can I do? I thought desperately. *I've got nothing!* But ready or not, this was my moment of truth. In that instant, Bigelow's voice echoed in my mind.

You have triumphed before, and you shall do so again.

I bit my lip, and tightened my grip on the RevealeR.

"Okay, here goes nothing," I whispered.

I dove right between the glowing blob and Timmy, and shined the sparse light of my flashlight squarely at the monster. A horrible wail erupted from the blob, echoing loudly through the room, and its glow grew even brighter. As I raised my hand to shield my eyes, one of the monster's tentacles wrapped itself around my arm and pulled me toward that shimmering mass.

"I...I'm being sucked in!" I shouted as I struggled to stay back. I reached out blindly for something to grab on to, and my hand found Timmy's arm.

"Don't worry! I've got you!" Timmy cried out as he grasped tightly on to my sleeve. "Hold on!"

As our grip on each other firmed, the light from my RevealeR suddenly flared, and fizzy blue streaks joined the beam. At that very moment, the glimmering blob squealed, then its pulsing light died and the glow surrounding it slowly faded. The monster's pull on me weakened, and I drew back and squinted hard.

"There...there's something *in* there..." I called out. "There's something inside the glowing blob!"

And as its blinding aura grew faint, the form within became apparent. It was a dark figure about six feet tall, with a broad chest and short, stocky arms filling out a navy blue sweatsuit. Its head was covered with a short, wavy mess of thinning red hair.

"D...Daddy?" Timmy mumbled. His hand dropped from my sleeve, and the light from my RevealeR immediately faded and lost its bluish tint. "Daddy? It's *you*?"

"Your dad?" I said. "What is it about fathers? *My* monster was my dad too."

But Timmy didn't answer. Neither did the monster that looked like his father. I shined my RevealeR in his

143

face, but it had no effect on him: he just turned and walked casually toward the phone on Timmy's desk.

"It was *him*," I surmised. "He must have been the one that left the monster prints on the phone."

I turned back to Timmy, who was staring at the monster with his mouth hanging open. He was drooling onto his chin, but somehow it seemed like a bad time for me to point that out.

"Timmy!" I shouted, shaking him to get his attention. "What does he do? What does your dad say on the phone that scares you so much?"

"What?" he replied dazedly. "I...I don't know what you're talking about."

"You don't...?" But then I froze. Timmy's father-monster had reached the desk upon which the phone sat, but when he reached down to pick up the receiver, the loud, shrieking voice echoed through the room again.

"No!" it wailed. "Mine!"

"Wha..." I muttered. "Who...?"

Suddenly, the air around us grew bright with streaks of orange and red. I scanned the room searching for the source and spotted the golden ring, still hovering near the desk. It was now enflamed with a burning halo, and the golden glow surrounding it had been replaced by crimson fires. The sparkling rays that erupted from its center turned into shooting flames, and spears of fire began to strike all around us.

"Run!" Timmy cried as he stumbled back. "Head for the fort!"

"No!" I shouted, grabbing him by the shirt and pulling him back. "You have to stand up to it..."

At just that moment, I screamed as a burst of flame shot through the air and scorched my shoulder, burning a huge, searing hole in my jacket. I looked down at my smoldering coat, and then up at Timmy, who was still tangled in my grasp. We stared blankly at each other for a second as the smoke from my jacket circled our heads.

"Um, new plan," I muttered as more jets of fire shot out at us. "Run for your life!!!"

Timmy and I dove for cover just as flames engulfed the spot where we had been standing. We positioned ourselves behind the upright mattress, then turned back to see what was happening. As we stared in rapt horror, Timmy's father was blasted head-on by a spear of fire. He spun away, stumbled, and then staggered blindly backward. When he finally turned around to face us, we both recoiled in terror.

"Oh god..." Timmy howled. "Oh, no! *Daddyyyy!*"

For the figure swaying before us no longer bore a face, just a gaping, charred hole that stretched from ear to ear. An awful green slime began slowly seeping from the ragged flesh that encircled the wound.

"I think I'm going to puke," I moaned.

But as if that wasn't enough to send us running for the nearest bathroom, things got even worse. A set of giant fangs suddenly grew out of that oozing hole, and then the monster straightened up and began taking stumbling steps in our direction. Timmy cowered and backed away, but I held my ground and turned my flashlight on the creature, pointing its weak, fizzy beam as steadily as my shaking hands would allow. But the bubbles of light seemed to bounce right off, and the monster kept growing.

"I'm sorry, but he can't come to the phone at the moment," spoke the terrible, shrieking voice, which seemed to come from all around us.

"Timmy!" I called back without looking, keeping my eyes and my light fixed squarely on the monster in front of me. But its horrible, slimy fangs kept growing nearer. "Timmy, that voice...it's not coming from this monster! Whose voice is that, Timmy? If it's not your dad, whose voice is it?"

"Put him on the phone!" Timmy's voice echoed through the room. "Put him on right now!"

"Put him on the phone?" I asked puzzledly, turning quickly to look at Timmy. "What does..."

But when I saw Timmy's face, it was frozen in a terrified whimper. As I watched, he began shaking his head back and forth and silently mouthed the words, "No, no, no..."

"That voice..." I realized, "That was your voice, Timmy. But it wasn't *you* speaking, was it?"

Timmy shook his head.

"But if the voice didn't come from you," I reasoned, "and it didn't come from *me*, then..."

As I spoke, my RevealeR began to whirr. Its light flickered, and the bubble-like stream turned the color of a tropical sea. The monster in front of me, with fangs that now stretched from the top of its burned-out head to its scorched, blackened chin, staggered a moment, but then kept advancing. I pointed my RevealeR right at the slimy hole that used to be its face, but it did not shrink or slow down. I looked down at my RevealeR, and then back up at that slimy mess.

"You..." I said to the monster, "You're not the one..."

146

Then I looked over at the ring, which continued to hover and shoot fiery rays from across the room. I hesitated a moment, but then I turned my RevealeR from the monster in front of me and pointed it at the ring. It instantly stopped shooting flames and began shaking. And then...

"Put him on!" the Timmy-like voice repeated. The ring vibrated in tune with the sound. "You put him on the phone! I know he's there!"

The *real* Timmy shuddered, and wrapped his arms around his shoulders.

"Daddy, no," he whimpered to himself. "Daddy, please come home and save me."

And then, as I watched Timmy shiver as though he was sitting on a block of ice, it finally hit me.

"Timmy...your father, he... he doesn't live here anymore, does he?'

"He does!" Timmy shouted. "He's just been working late a lot! He'll be coming home!"

But in spite of Timmy's denial, my RevealeR grew warm in my hand, and its beam began to pulse. Somehow, I knew that I was on the right track.

"Are your parents...getting divorced?" I asked in as gentle a tone as I could.

I guess Jeannine was right about me not being very tactful, because that made Timmy lose it.

"NO!" he screeched, grabbing me with both hands. "No they're just...sorting things out, that's all. My dad will come home soon! He promised!"

And then Timmy did the worst thing he could possibly do. He started crying.

Guys, back me up on this.

Well, with Timmy clinging to my shirt, crying, my flashlight still dim, and a slimy monster with giant fangs about to devour us alive, I was pretty much bummed out. I tried pointing my RevealeR at the monster again, but the beam was repelled like water off a duck's back.

"Jeannine," I called out weakly. "This would be a really good time to rub two sticks together."

The monster finally reached the mattress that stood between us and in one swift motion flung it aside like my dad tossing his laundry when he's searching for a clean pair of socks. It rose above us, its hideous fangs dripping with green slime, and prepared to strike.

Chapter Twenty - Illuminations

It should come as no shock that at that moment my survival instincts were begging me to abandon Timmy and run for it. But like a true hero (or a complete idiot, depending on your point of view) I firmed my stance. I tried to push Timmy back, but he was as stiff as a statue, and just about as heavy. The monster's arms flailed blindly, and when its jaws chomped at us I smacked it in the teeth with my flashlight. It wasn't a very effective club, but at that point it wasn't of much other use either. The monster roared angrily, then grabbed me by the shirt and pulled me toward its slimy fangs...

At that very moment, the door to Timmy's room burst open and in strode Jeannine, flashlight in hand.

"Take this, you creep!" she bellowed as she flicked the switch and shined her light on the beast. Her RevealeR purred like the engine of a race car, and the pinkish stream that burst from it was bright and strong. The monster screeched, dropped its hold on me, and fell back. It cowered, and started swinging its arms wildly

as if to fight off the beam. I picked myself up from where the monster had dropped me, rubbed my bruised head where it had banged against the desk when I fell, and stepped over to Jeannine.

"Took your sweet time about it, didn't you?" I complained.

"I wasn't sure you really needed me," she said casually.

"Drama Queen," I grumbled as I turned back to the monster, which shrieked, and began shaking violently.

"Look," Timmy said. "It...it..."

"It's shrinking," I confirmed.

"Hold this!" Jeannine instructed as she tried forcing her flashlight into my hand.

"What? Why?" I protested.

"Just hold it!" she insisted as she shoved it into my fingers, and then hurried over to Timmy. Once her RevealeR transferred from her hand to mine, its beam began to dim.

"Um, I think it likes *you* better," I mumbled as the light faded. Darkness closed in on us, and the monster began to grow again. It rose and turned toward us.

"Jeannine, we have a problem!" I called out. But Jeannine ignored me. She always picks the worst times to do that.

"Timmy!" she said as she bent down to him. "Timmy, everything will be okay. My mom and dad got divorced too."

"No!" he cried. "My mom and dad are not..."

"Timmy, I was scared too. But you know what? Things are much better now. My mom and dad are both happier. And now I don't hear them yelling at each other all the time."

That was when I finally understood what had happened earlier when Jeannine ran from the room in terror.

"Jeannine," I said. "You couldn't stand looking at Timmy's ring monster because it was one of *your* buried fears too, wasn't it?"

Jeannine's neck stiffened as if from a sudden chill, but then she slowly nodded.

"Um, sorry about calling you a...you know, a *girl*," I said.

"*Later*," she hissed, and turned back to Timmy, who still cowered, sobbing. "Timmy, things are much better now. Even though my dad's not living with me anymore, I know he still loves me."

"No!" Timmy cried. "No, it's all a lie! He said he'd always be here when I need him. Well, I need him *now*! So where is he?"

At that, Jeannine fell back.

"I...I don't know..." she said. "Maybe...maybe he..."

"No! It was just a lie!" Timmy insisted. "He's never there for me! And I bet *your* dad is never there for you either!"

"N-no...it's not true," Jeannine mumbled, but then she fell into a sitting position and looked up, her eyes turning damp and glassy. The monster seemed to sense their growing despair, and began staggering toward them, groping frantically in their direction like someone on a diet reaching desperately for a hot fudge sundae.

"No!" I cried out as I leapt over to Timmy and Jeannine and jumped in front of the monster. "Leave her alone!" I shined both RevealeRs on the monster, but the light did not slow it down. Jeannine grabbed ahold of Timmy's sleeve as the monster drew ever closer.

If ever I needed to do some quick thinking, this was the time.

No, he can't come to the phone at the moment? Why was that so terrifying? Did that mean something terrible had happened, and Timmy couldn't reach his dad for help?

"No," I thought out loud. "Then why would Timmy purposely leave phones off the hook?" I looked at Timmy and Jeannine, cowering as the monster grew gigantic and rose above us.

"He doesn't *want* to reach his dad," I realized. "He doesn't want to hear..."

152

No, he can't come to the phone at the moment. But maybe Timmy hadn't been calling his dad's *office*...

"Timmy, does your dad have...a girlfriend?"

"Nooooooo!" he wailed. "No, he's going to come home! He's going to come save me from the monster!"

My flashlight suddenly whined and lit like fire, and Jeannine's, which was still in my other hand, grew bright again too. But before I could move, the monster's flailing arms swooped in and grabbed me, pinning my arms to my sides, and then it began lifting me toward its terrible fangs.

"Will! Oh, no!" Jeannine cried. "You...you stop that, you stupid monster! Leave him alone! Are you listening to me? I said leave him alone!"

Leave it to Jeannine to think she could defeat a monster by nagging it to death. As for me, I knew that there was no time left for asking any more questions. A cold terror washed over me as I was drawn toward that face full of glistening daggers, and I squirmed and tugged as the monster pulled me in closer. Finally, I managed to tear one arm free.

"I think I understand now," I said as I stared into that slimy maw, "S-so...so take this!" And I turned the beam from my flashlight back onto the monster.

"Come on!" I urged, shaking my RevealeR desperately. "I need you to work...NOW!"

Only nothing happened. My RevealeR just wheezed, and the monster's face turned into a ghastly, hair to chin, ear to ear grin as it drew me toward its mouth. I was so close that the slime from its teeth dripped on my face...

Now I don't mind telling you, my body was so bursting with fear that it shook like our car did the day my dad poured brake fluid where the oil was supposed to go. But at just that moment, I heard Bigelow's voice in the back of my brain once more.

Fear grips the body along with the mind, he had told me. *Steadying your breathing will calm your body and help clear your mind. Then you can see past the fear and focus on the task at hand.*

My breaths were coming in fits and gasps, but I had been too focused on keeping my head from becoming the monster's chew toy to pay much attention to that.

"Calm my breathing," I gasped to myself. "I'll try."

154

So even as I struggled to keep the monster from chowing down on my face, I tried to inhale as deeply and slowly as I could.

Focus, I thought to myself. *See past the fear.*

"I can do this..." I whispered. "I can do this..." I forced down another deep, slow breath, and as my breathing steadied, it was like a fog began to lift from my brain. Unfortunately, my brain, along with the rest of my head, was very near to entering the monster's throat. But as the fog faded, I felt a warmth deep inside me – the same warmth I felt when I held my Teddy. It spread through my body, and poured into my fingers. A powerful humming sound suddenly surged from my RevealeR, and its light flared brightly. The beam struck dead center on the monster's face, and its entire form started shaking and writhing. The ghastly grin faded, turning to a scowl of rage. I pointed the light right into the monster's slimy jaws, and it shrieked with fury. Then, incredibly, that horrible face melted into a mass of churning goo. The monster's grip on me weakened, and I squirmed to slip free.

"Timmy," I called out as I dropped back to the floor. "This will hurt, but you've got to face the monster. If you don't, it will never leave you."

"Noooooooo!" he cried. "After what it almost did to *you*? I can't!"

"Timmy," Jeannine said. "I couldn't look at it either. But maybe we can do it together! We can be braver together!" And she tugged on Timmy's arm, making him rise, reluctantly, to his feet.

"Come on!" she prodded. "We can do it." And then she gave him a gentle nudge, urging him to look.

"Hey!" I complained as I stepped over beside her and handed her back her flashlight. "How come he gets a little nudge, but I always get my foot stomped on?"

She just stomped my foot again.

"Owww!" I bellowed as I hopped in pain. Jeannine then turned back to Timmy, nodded, and together they looked up at the monster.

"There!" Jeannine said encouragingly. "This isn't so bad!"

"It...it's horrible..." Timmy said weakly, shielding his eyes as though he was looking into the sun.

"It *is* horrible," I agreed, as I straightened up and turned to face that grotesque, slimy monster again. "But it's not the one."

"Not...the one?" Timmy mumbled.

"Not the one behind it all," I answered. "This isn't your Hidden Beast. I understand that now." And then I lifted my RevealeR and pointed its beam back at the monster. The light was strong, much brighter than it had been before, and when it struck the monster, it fell back and began to glow again. Its form turned molten, and melted back into a shimmering blob. Then it started to shrink.

"I knew it!" I shouted triumphantly. "This monster is just a decoy that your Hidden Beast, the monster that's causing all this, threw out at us to shield itself! My own Hidden Beast did the same thing!"

"Then...then what is *my* Hidden Beast?" Timmy asked.

"I, um..." I mumbled, as the light from my RevealeR suddenly began to flicker.

"I think *I* know," Jeannine said. And with that she stepped forward and lifted her RevealeR. Her light was strong and bright, far brighter than mine, and when it fell on the monster, it shrieked, and its shrinking, molten form shriveled and surged violently. Strangely though, the glow surrounding it grew stronger, and then the blob started slowly dissolving back into the light. Jeannine smiled.

"This monster-fighting stuff is no big deal," she said. "My drama coach makes me work harder than this."

But at that very moment, Timmy shuddered, lifting a finger to point at the glowing mass.

"L...look," he whispered as his hand shook in front of him. "S-something's happening..."

And he was right. Behind the shrinking, squirming blob, a new form began to take shape within the light. Just then, the shrill, echoing monster-voice erupted around us once more.

"No, your father can't come to the phone at the moment," it shrieked. "He's...busy right now."

"You put him on! I want to talk to him!" We heard Timmy cry out.

Only it *wasn't* Timmy. Jeannine and I turned and looked right at him, but he was completely frozen, and hadn't uttered a word.

"You put him on right now!" insisted Timmy's voice.

"That...that's Timmy's voice," Jeannine said. "But where is it coming from?"

"Hel*lo* Jeannine," I grumbled. "It's not coming from me, you, or Timmy. Where do you *think* it's coming from?"

"You mean," she gasped. "The voice is coming from the *monster itself?*"

157

"Obviously," I said impatiently. "The real question is *WHY*? Whatever Timmy's Hidden Beast is, it sent that daddy-monster and is using those voices to try and scare us off. But why did the monster think hearing that would be frightening?"

"Um..." Jeannine stuttered. "I...I think we may be about to find out. Look."

Jeannine pointed over my shoulder, and I turned back to look at the glowing blob. From its silvery form, something reached out to us. Glistening fingers pierced the surface, and then hands, shiny like the face of a mirror, poked through. Finally, as we stared spellbound at the sight, a new horror began to emerge.

Chapter Twenty-one - Breakdowns

"Something..." Timmy stuttered as he reached out and tugged on my sleeve. "Something is coming..."

"I can see that!" I grumbled irritably as I pulled loose from his grasp and turned to face the figure emerging from the glowing mass. The dazzling form was smaller than Timmy's father had been, but was more radiant, with sparkles of light shimmering all over.

"Wow..." I mumbled in an almost trance-like voice, "It's so...beautiful."

But just then Timmy grabbed my arm again. When I looked back and saw the terror in his eyes, I remembered where I was, and what I was facing. Without another word, I lifted my RevealeR and pointed it at the glistening form. The aura around it immediately flickered, and its glow grew soft and diffuse. Slowly, the glare faded, until at last the figure within was revealed.

It was a woman. Not a horrible, monster-looking kind of woman, mind you. A *gorgeous* woman. She was tall, blond, and perfectly tan, wearing a glittery gold halter top, a short black skirt, fancy high-heel shoes, and lots of big, flashy jewelry.

"That's *it*?" I wondered out loud. "Your terrifying monster is some kind of a...a fashion model? What are you afraid she'll do, give you a makeover?"

But both Jeannine and Timmy were positively horrified. I stared in shock at their eyes, which were wide and frozen with fear.

"I don't..." I muttered as I gazed from one terror-stricken face to the other, "I don't get it..."

Don't be mad at Will, Jeannine had told Timmy. *He just doesn't know what it's like.*

"Bigelow said I need to understand the monster to make the RevealeR work," I whispered to myself. "But what can I do if I don't..."

But at that very moment, my eyes caught sight of the RevealeR in Jeannine's hand, whose bright beam was pointing uselessly at the ceiling.

"Of course!" I shouted, and then ran over to Jeannine and shook her arm hard until I drew her eyes over to mine.

"Jeannine! Shine your light on the monster! It has to be *you* that does it!"

"What difference will that make?" she growled angrily, pulling her arm away.

"It makes *all* the difference!" I insisted. "I don't fully understand the monster, so I can't really see it the way Timmy does. But *you* do. We need your light! You have to show me what the monster looks like to you!"

Jeannine glared at me, but then turned her gaze back to the monster, and her face hardened. She lifted her RevealeR and pointed the beam right at the monster in high-heel shoes.   But instead of brightening, the monster's face grew dark, and its soft, glowing features turned stiff and sharp.

"That's it!" I shouted. "I'm finally starting to see!"

But what I started to see was dreadful.   The shimmering, golden curls on her head turned filthy and shaggy, and spiked horns sprouted from her suddenly weed-like hair. Her fingers stretched longer and became rigid, pointy talons, and her arms turned dark and scaly. Her body melted and morphed into the shape of a demonic gargoyle, except for her feet, which turned orange and duck-like. They actually looked kind of comical, but I suppose when your mouth is filled with three-inch fangs no one makes fun of your feet.

"It..." I stuttered. "It's a...a HARPY!"

As I watched, the monster lifted her hand and the telephone receiver floated into her grasp, then a voice, shrill and full of venom, erupted into the air.

"I told you he's busy!" the monster said smugly into the receiver. "I'll have him call you back when he can." Then a twisted, evil grin spread across her face.

"Or, will I?" she added, and then cackled a hideous, shrieking laugh.   I gasped when her open mouth revealed a slithering, serpent tongue, and rows of shark-like teeth.

"NO!" Timmy cried out. I waved my hand in front of Timmy's mouth to be sure it was really him talking. He smacked it away.

"NO! You can't have him! He's mine!" Timmy cried.

"Oh, really?" the monster said.

161

She produced from behind her back her other hand, which she opened to reveal a six-inch high figure of...

"Daddy, no!" Timmy cried. "Don't let her! Don't let her take you!"

I turned to Jeannine, whose hands were shaking. The monster giggled, dropped the receiver, and then took Timmy's father and began twisting and turning him like he was made of silly putty. She stretched and pulled, and then finally wrapped him around her little finger, prodding his head so that it bounced up and down like a bungee ball. Jeannine let out a huge sob, then dropped her flashlight and fell whimpering to the floor. Timmy cowered, and the monster, no longer bathed in the light of Jeannine's RevealeR, began to grow. She quickly towered over me, and her claw-like fingers poised to strike.

"Um, guys, I could use a little help here..." I whispered as the monster rose above me.

"Now then, where was I?" the monster posed. "Ah, yesss..." And with that, she let out an ear-piercing shriek, unfurled a pair of bat-like wings, and took to the air. She hovered briefly, then plunged at me, swiping her claws viciously. I dove aside in the nick of time. The monster let out another shrieking laugh.

"Timmy!" I shouted. "You have to stand up to this thing! You have to face it, Timmy!"

But Timmy and Jeannine continued cowering, and did not get up.

It's no use, I thought. *He's too scared. We **all** are.*

Things were looking pretty bad, but at just that moment, I heard Bigelow's voice once more in the back of my head.

Remember, Will: things are always less scary when you face them with a friend.

He...he didn't mean himself, I realized. *He meant us. He meant NOW!*

"Timmy! Jeannine!" I shouted as I ran over to them. "Grab hold! Grab hold of my flashlight!"

I held it out to Timmy, but he recoiled like I was handing him one of my mother's goat's milk ice cream bars. I turned to Jeannine, but she pulled away.

"Jeannine!" I pleaded. "Jeannine, grab hold! We can only beat this thing together!"

Jeannine sobbed, and then looked up at me with tearstained eyes.

"I...I can't, Will!" she cried. "You were right. I'm not brave enough. I'm just a *girl*."

"You *are* brave! And you were right! You were right all along! I *need* you! We all need each other! We can be braver together!"

I pushed the flashlight toward her, and she tentatively reached for it. When she touched it, its hum turned melodic, almost like a song, and the beam grew stronger, with streaks of fizzy pink bubbles joining its greenish stream. Jeannine looked up at me, and I nodded. She grabbed hold firmly.

"Now you, Timmy!" I called out. "We all have to do this together!"

Timmy whimpered, but Jeannine reached out and touched him gently on the shoulder. He gazed at her, and her calm eyes drew him closer. Together, Jeannine and I held out the light to him, and he took hold. As he grasped the shaft, a swirl of powerful blue streaks intensified the beam.

Just then...

"Well, what have we here?" the shrieking harpy bellowed. "Fresh meat?!" And then she flapped her wings and flew right at us.

"Stay cool," I instructed as Timmy and Jeannine shook with fear. "Breathe with me."

"Say *what?*" Timmy sputtered.

"Breathe like I do! Breathe deeply to help calm yourself, and then we can focus on showing this witch for what she really is!"

And we did. The three of us stood together and took a long, deep breath. Then we held fast to my RevealeR, and pointed it true.

The monster screamed. She dropped from the air and began writhing on the floor, shriveling and

164

shrinking as she hissed and snapped at us. The figure of Timmy's father, which still dangled in the palm of her claw, unraveled, and began to grow. In seconds, it was larger than the monster that held it, whose grip on him weakened in the glow from the RevealeR.

"Yes!" Timmy cheered.

"It's working!" Jeannine shouted. "Will, you're doing it!"

"*We're* doing it," I corrected. "Together, we have enough bravery and understanding to finally reveal the truth about this monster!"

And even as I spoke, a monster's voice erupted into the air around us. But the voice was not a screech or shriek anymore.

"He hates me," a soft, echoing woman's voice moaned. "Your son hates me."

"He doesn't hate you," a calm, though exasperated sounding man's voice resounded in reply. Timmy stiffened at the sound of the voice.

"He *really* hates me," the woman's voice maintained. "Every time I answer the phone..."

"Give the kid a break," the man coaxed. "He's had a really tough time with all that's been going on."

"Dad!" Timmy whispered as a slow smile crept onto his face. "Dad, you...you stood up for me!"

And though neither of the figures before us seemed to notice, the change in Timmy's mood strengthened the beam from the RevealeR, and its greenish tint turned to ocean blue. Then, as the scene continued playing out, the monsters slowly shrank.

"*He's* had a tough time?" The woman cried out, and for a moment a bit of the terrible screeching sound returned to her voice. "What about *me*? I never asked for any of this! I never asked for all of these complications and problems and sticky situations!"

As the voice rang out, the tiny harpy tried to slash and tear at the figure of Timmy's father, but her talons had no effect. She hissed and clawed at him, but he remained firm and impassive.

"Like it or not, you *chose* all that when you chose to be with me," Timmy's father countered. "But Timmy didn't get to choose, yet his whole world has been turned upside-down. And it's all been too much for him."

"So that makes it okay for him to treat me like...like I'm some horrible creature?" the woman hissed.

"Look, what do you think I can do?" Timmy's dad protested. "We're already sending him to a therapist. What more do you want?"

"I want him to stop hating me!" the woman cried. "I want him to..."

"He doesn't hate you," the man insisted. "He doesn't even know you. All he sees is a woman who broke up his family and stole away his daddy."

"*What*?! I hadn't even *met* you then!" the woman shouted indignantly. "I didn't have anything to do with you and your wife breaking up!"

"I know that," Timmy's father said impatiently. "But Timmy doesn't. Not yet. But he'll come around. He's a good kid. Just give it time."

Just give it time. Those words bounced around the room, and Timmy grew stronger, and his posture grew straighter with every echo. As Timmy firmed, the monsters weakened and shrank more, until they were the size of two action figures.

"You see, Timmy?" I coaxed. "Just keep facing them! In the light of truth, the monsters can't hurt you."

But at that very moment, the doll-sized harpy turned from the image of Timmy's father and faced us once more, her fangs still bared and vicious.

"Oh, you think so?" the tiny figure taunted. Her voice, unlike the soft woman's voice that had spoken to Timmy's father, was still a monstrous shriek. "You don't think I have a few tricks left?"

A sudden surge of burning heat shot through my hand where it gripped the RevealeR, and a reddish burst flared through its beam. I looked up at Timmy, and I saw anger blazing in his eyes. I turned my gaze back to the harpy and kept the RevealeR pointed at her, steady and sure, and she continued shrinking.

"There's much more to fear than just little old me, isn't there?" the demonic woman teased as she shrank. "Wouldn't you agree, Timmy?"

"Huh!" I said smugly. "I wonder what she meant by *that*?"

Just then, Jeannine stomped on my foot again.

"Yeeooww!" I yelled. "What do you think you're doing?"

But Jeannine just pointed behind me, and when I turned around, a chill ran up my spine. The monster-woman had told the truth: there was definitely something more to fear.

Much more.

Chapter Twenty-two – Trappings

Timmy, Jeannine, and I stood gaping at what we saw. There, hovering over by the desk, was the ring. Only it wasn't a little, slip-onto-your-finger golden band any more. It was a huge, blazing hoop, bigger than a beach ball, and was still swelling enormously. In just seconds, it was bigger than Timmy's mattress-fort.

"It...it's growing," I muttered.

"Duh, Sherlock," Jeannine hissed.

"But...but why?" I wondered. "It's just a ring!"

I pulled my RevealeR away from Jeannine and Timmy and shined its light on the ring, but it had no effect. The ring kept growing, and as it did, it rose above us, continuing to expand in the empty space over our heads. It quickly filled the room, stretching almost from wall to wall.

"What is it doing...?" I started to say. But before I could utter even one more word, the ring dropped down, descending until it completely surrounded us.

"Noooooooo!" Timmy wailed. "No, let me out!"

"There's no way out!" I shouted as I whirled about, shining my RevealeR in every direction. "We're trapped!"

I spun around, but my light revealed nothing but the shimmering inner walls of the ring. A cackling laugh drew my eyes back to the doll-size harpy. She bared her fangs and hissed at me, but then melted back into a molten blob and dissolved into the golden band surrounding us. The giant barrier then churned, and the quivering walls sprouted bulbs. They grew long and snake-like, becoming golden tentacles that waved through the air blindly.

"I have a bad feeling about this…" Timmy mumbled.

Meanwhile, from the spot on the ring into which the harpy-monster had melted, another glowing blob emerged. It was much like the first one, except that its oblong form was horizontal, and it radiated…I don't know, *hunger*. But it remained no more than a blob: fluid and formless. At least, that's how it appeared to *me*.

"That looks like…" Jeannine whispered as she rummaged through her pocket for her glasses and threw them on. "Oh! Oh, *NO*!"

"What?" I called out as I moved in to examine the blob closer. "What is it? What do you see?"

But before she could answer, some of the golden tentacles suddenly swung in front of me. I tried stepping around them, but they encircled the blob, cutting me off. The ends of the tentacles then poked at me, pushing me away.

"Call me crazy," Timmy suggested. "But I think they're trying to tell you to back off."

"Hah! I'm not letting some overgrown golden spaghetti hold me back," I said, smacking away the arms like I was carving a path through dense jungle vines.

"Um, I don't know, Will," Timmy cautioned. "Don't you think that they might..."

But even as he spoke, the feelers I had swatted away swung back at me, and then the ends of the tentacles swelled like an inflating balloon. Suddenly, the golden bubbles burst, and headless, fanged jaws sprouted from within. The fang-tipped tentacles hissed and swayed in every direction, and took monstrous bites at the air all around us, forcing us all to dodge and retreat.

"Smooth move, Mr. Monster Detective!" Timmy cried as he jumped and sidestepped the flying teeth. "What do we do *now*?"

"Um, I'm working on it!" I shouted as I ducked a set of snapping jaws.

To be perfectly honest, at that moment I was running kind of low in the ideas department. But though I was at a loss for what to do next, Jeannine turned resolute.

"I'll show this monster that it can't... uh, wait," she shouted, but then began feeling around her clothes frantically for something in her pocket that was not there. "Oh, this stupid dress! Where's my flashlight?"

"The same place as everything else you lose!" I hollered. "It's right in front of you!"

Jeannine looked down and spotted her yellow, flower-covered flashlight on the ground, lying where she had dropped it earlier. She reached to grab it, but several sets of fangs snapped at her, driving her back. Suddenly, more long, slimy tentacles grew from the wall behind Jeannine, and they reached to snare her.

"No!" I cried, and leaped between Jeannine and the tentacles, which then grabbed me like an octopus. I struggled against those slimy arms, but one of them wrapped itself around my leg, and the next thing I knew, it had hoisted me right off the ground and hung me upside down like side of beef in a meat locker.

"Oh, how do I get myself into these things?" I grumbled as a pair of vicious, fanged jaws came flying right at my face.

That's right, this is where my story started. But if you think that how I ended up like that makes for a strange story, believe me, things were still just getting interesting.

"Will! Look out!" Jeannine shouted as I swayed back and forth, dodging and swiping at the incoming jaws.

"Just get the light!" I yelled back as I smacked one set of fangs with the casing of my RevealeR. But just then, another tentacle reached to grab her.

171

"No! Get back!" I heard Timmy's voice shout as he jumped in and flailed and fought with the advancing arm. He looked around frantically and spotted something perched against a stack of books nearby.

"My hockey stick!" he roared. "Perfect!" He dashed over and grabbed it, then began swinging it wildly at the tentacles and the flying jaws. He smacked one pair of fangs right into next week.

"Ha!" He shouted. "Gotcha!" But even as he spoke, more tendrils began sprouting, and it was just a matter of time before they ensnared us all. Jeannine looked back at me desperately.

"Go!" I shouted.

Give Jeannine credit, she didn't hesitate. She ducked under the tentacles, dodged the snapping teeth, and dove to grab her RevealeR. She picked it up, and sighed.

"Well, that's more like it..." But before she could finish her sentence, one of the tendrils grabbed her and lifted her upside down off the floor, making her dress hang down over her face.

"Jeannine, use the light!" I called out as a pair of fangs bit into my jacket and began shaking me, drawing me closer to those hideous teeth.

"I can't!" she moaned as she tried to push her dress back up her legs. "You'll...you'll see my panties!"

"Jeannine!" I shouted. "I'm getting *eaten* here!" My right arm and my one free leg were braced against the slobbering fangs, straining to prevent them from snapping shut on me.

"Oh, all right!" she grumbled, her voice slightly muffled by the portion of her dress that had floated in front of her face. She flicked on the switch. Light roared out of her RevealeR like a raging river, and when Jeannine pointed it at the walls of the giant ring, the sound of screeching instantly filled the air. The tendrils began to melt, and the snapping jaws withdrew back into the wall.

"Yeeeooow!" I cried as the dissolving tentacle dropped me, and I fell just like a sack of potatoes. Except potatoes don't get bruised when they land on their heads. Meanwhile, the tentacle holding Jeannine let her down gently before fading away.

"Girls always have it easier," I grumbled as I rubbed the swelling lump on the back of my skull.

"Oh, stop whining," Jeannine retorted. "It was only your head." I glared at her, but Jeannine's eyes were fixed upon the melting, morphing inner walls of the ring, which flattened and grew taller, until they looked like the inside of a doll's house. I began staring at them too, but waves of screeching noises kept buffeting my ears, and I finally turned to find their source. It seemed that they were coming from the glowing, oblong blob, but when I pointed my RevealeR at it, nothing happened.

"This makes no sense," I said, noticing as I spoke that my light had dimmed once more. "We uncovered the truth about Timmy's monster, and he faced it. The harpy lost her power. So what is *this*? I don't get it."

"Don't you?" Jeannine chided, glancing down her nose at me with an annoying *I know something you don't know* look on her face. "Obviously, that harpy wasn't the one we were looking for." And then she turned the beam of her RevealeR to the glowing blob. But nothing happened.

"Okay," I muttered. "What am I supposed to be seeing, exactly?"

But even though *I* didn't notice any difference, Timmy went nuts. He held his ears and began swinging around like he was being whipped from every direction.

"Nooooooo!" he shouted. "Make it stop!"

"Jeannine!" I yelled. "I don't know what you're doing, but it isn't working! Nothing is happening!"

"Yes it is!"

"It is?" I squinted. "What are you talking about?" I swung around and scanned in every direction again, but everything still looked the same. But as I stared at Timmy, flailing wildly as with his hands cupped tightly to his ears, I suddenly realized that even though what I was *seeing* hadn't changed, what I was *hearing* had.

"The screeching..." I whispered. "It's changed. It's more of a...a wail..."

"It's crying," Jeannine corrected.

"Crying?" I sputtered. "The monster is *crying*? What kind of monster...?"

Then, like a ton of bricks, it hit me. The light of my RevealeR suddenly burned bright again. I knew.

"It...it *can't* be..."

But as I waved the beam of my RevealeR around the room, everything began coming into focus. The walls of the ring were no longer just a glowing blur. Details became clear, and decorations came into view: lacy curtains, turquoise and pink wallpaper with patterns of bears and bunnies, and in the corner of the room, a rocking horse. I turned the beam back to the oblong blob and its glow faded, and the monster within was revealed. After all of our battles and ordeals, the final horror, Timmy's true Hidden Beast, faced us at last.

Chapter Twenty-three – Nurseries

It looked like a small, topless cage on stilts. Along the inside of the bars ran a frilly white bumper that blocked any view of what was within. The sides rustled as though something inside was shaking back and forth.

"A crib?" I puzzled. "Timmy's Hidden Beast is a..."

At just that moment, another deafening wail roared at us, so loud that the crib and surrounding furniture shook like they were in an earthquake. My legs wobbled and I struggled to keep my balance, but after I righted myself and saw what had caused the noise, my knees started shaking from the *inside*.

You see, the sides of the crib rustled once more, only this time something reached out. A huge hand, petite and swollen like a baby's, but grime-covered and purplish with horrid scales and spines, rose into view above the top of the bumper.

"Eeeuuuuuww!" Jeannine sputtered disgustedly. "Don't monsters believe in personal hygiene?"

Just then a sharp, piercing cry rang out that rattled the walls.

"**FEED ME!**" it shrieked.

And with that, there was a harsh tearing noise as the bumper around the crib was shredded into a gazillion pieces. Then something behind the shreds arose. I say *something* because I honestly couldn't guess what it was. It looked like a giant, beaten-up soccer ball that had fallen into a toxic waste dump. But then it rotated toward me, and two horrid, bulging red eyes stared down at us. Its nose was just a moss-covered stump, and its mouth was barely visible through the goo that covered the entire head. Until it opened that is, revealing massive, slime-covered fangs.

"**FEED ME!**" the thing in the crib bellowed.

I looked over at Timmy.

"Um, do you still have those chocolate bars?" I asked weakly. Timmy didn't answer, unless you consider squeaking like a cornered mouse to be a form of response. Meanwhile, the monster didn't wait for us to provide what it wanted. Its horrible mouth cracked open wide, and a frog-like tongue shot out in our direction.

"Look out!" I shouted as I lunged at Jeannine and shoved her aside. We dove down, and the tongue soared past us and flew straight at Timmy.

"Timmy, move!" I yelled. But he just stood there like a deer frozen in headlights. The tongue snared the end of Timmy's hockey stick, and then yanked it right out of his hands and pulled it back to the monster-baby's mouth. Its horrible jaws snapped the stick in two, and then drew it into its mouth, where it began noisily chewing. Once the stick was gone, the monster let out a thunderous belch, and the entire room vibrated.

"**FEED ME!**" it said again, looking down at Timmy hungrily like he was a giant Hershey Bar.

"Timmy!" I called to him. "Timmy, snap out of it!" But he just stared blankly at the monster as its tongue shot out again. But this time the tongue wasn't aimed at Timmy. Instead, it snared the doll-sized figure of Timmy's father.

"**No, let me go!**" the figure howled. It struggled and squirmed helplessly as the tongue drew it toward those horrible, grinding teeth. Timmy moaned a wail of despair.

"Noooooo!" he cried, finally breaking out of his stupor and running over to the tiny figure of his father. He grabbed hold of one arm and began pulling, trying to yank his father loose, but the strength of the monster was too much for him, and he was dragged along with his father toward those terrible jaws.

"Jeannine!" I called out desperately. "Jeannine, use your light! I need to see what Timmy is really up against!"

"But I *am* using my light!" she shouted back.

"What?!" I bellowed, turning my head to look at her. Sure enough, she was right behind me, RevealeR in hand, with its beam pointed squarely at the monsters.

"But this makes no sense!" I protested.

"Doesn't it?!" Jeannine hollered impatiently. "Come on, Jimmy Neutron, boy genius! Figure it out!"

"You know I hate when people call me that!" I complained. "Can't you just use your light to show me what this looks like to you?"

"I *am* showing you!" she insisted.

"You...are...?" I mumbled. And I turned back to the monsters again. Timmy was still tugging desperately at his father's arm, trying to pull him loose, while the doll sized figure's legs were bracing against the ground, fighting the pull of the tongue that drew him relentlessly toward those crushing jaws.

"No!" Timmy cried out. "No, he's mine!" But still the tongue dragged both of them ever closer. The figure of Timmy's father reached the frame of the crib, and he tried to brace himself against the bars.

"Stop!" he cried out. "Let go! I have to go to Timmy!"

"**NO GO TO TIMMY!**" the monster yelled. "**DADDY MUST FEED ME!**"

"*Daddy* must..." I whispered to myself. "Of...of course!" As realization struck me, the light from my RevealeR instantly grew strong once more.

"You get it now?" Jeannine asked.

"Yes," I said. And with that, I pointed my RevealeR at the monster and shined the light right in its face. Instantly, its fangs and red eyes began melting away.

"That's it!" I cheered. "Now I...wait, something's wrong..."

Something *was* wrong. Really, *really* wrong. The monster wasn't shrinking at all. And even though its fangs were gone, the monstrous frog-like tongue remained, and continued to draw the figure of Timmy's father, kicking and screaming, to its mouth.

"Nooooo! Stop!" Timmy's father pleaded as his feet began to slide into the baby's jaws. "Stop this! Timmy needs me!" But he kept sliding in deeper. Timmy braced himself against the crib and pulled desperately

179

on the arm of his father, struggling to tear him from the monster-baby's jaws.

"What's going on?" I cried. "My RevealeR is having no effect!"

"Mine neither!" Jeannine shrieked. "Why isn't it working?"

"Noooooo!" Timmy screamed as the monster sucked his father's legs into its mouth and continued chewing. "Let go!" Then his eyes turned to me.

"Help me!" he begged. "Please, help!"

I watched Timmy struggling to pull his father free, and smacked my flashlight in frustration.

"Why won't it work?" I wondered helplessly.

It was then that I remembered my talk with Bigelow, and what I had learned about the RevealeR.

It shines light on monsters. It reveals the truth about them, and makes them less scary.

"It reveals the truth about the monsters," I whispered. "The RevealeR shows what Timmy is really scared of."

"What?" Jeannine said.

"Jeannine! I've got it! The light reveals the truth about Timmy's fear! That's what it does!"

"Yes," Jeannine muttered. "So what?"

"Well," I answered, "what if this *is* the truth?"

Jeannine gave me a *you've lost your mind* kind of look.

"The truth?" she said. "Timmy's afraid that his dad will be eaten by a baby monster is the *truth*?"

"No! But what if Timmy's father doesn't have much time for him anymore? Maybe his dad really is being taken from him!"

"By a baby?" Jeannine wondered.

180

"It's possible, isn't it?" I posed.

"Possible? Well, sure!" she said caustically. "I mean, *anything's* possible…"

Suddenly, Jeannine's eyes lit up. She looked down at her flashlight, and it grew brighter.

"Of course…" she whispered to herself. Then she turned back to me and bellowed, "Will! You said the RevealeR turns truth into light, right?"

"Right! But that's not doing us any good…"

"Well, there's more than just *one* truth possible here! Maybe we can use the RevealeR to make Timmy see some *other* truth! Let's show him a different possibility."

"And how do we do that?"

Jeannine bit her lip for a moment, then without another word she pointed her flashlight at the baby and closed her eyes.

"Take hold!" she commanded.

I hate when she gets all bossy like that, but it was the only plan going, so I did what she said.

"Okay!" I grumbled. "Now what?"

"Now close your eyes and try to think of something nice about having a new baby in your family!" she instructed.

"What? Why?" I asked. Jeannine shook her head impatiently, and I'm pretty sure that she rolled her eyes under her closed eyelids too.

"Will," she said. "You told me that if we understand something, the RevealeR can make light so that everyone will see it, right?"

"Right! Then we can all see what you see."

"Well then, if we understand that there are other possibilities besides this one," she explained, "maybe the light can show *them* to Timmy too."

For a moment, my mouth hung open stupidly. But at least I didn't drool.

"That...that's brilliant, Jeannine!" I gushed. "Let's try it!"

And so I closed my eyes and tried to imagine how much fun it would be to be a big brother. Unfortunately, the only images that came to my mind were of wailing babies, trashed toys, and poopy diapers.

"Um, I'm kind of drawing a blank here," I confessed. "Have you thought of anything? Anything *good* I mean?"

"I think so!" Jeannine called out. "Is it working?"

"I don't know," I replied. "Let me check."

And with that, I opened my eyes.

"Oh, wow..." I whispered. "I...I never expected *this*..."

For the room around us was now at war with itself. The monster nursery had begun to melt: the curtains, the rocking horse...everything but the crib and the daddy-chewing monster merged into an enveloping dark mass. Light and darkness attacked each other as the beam from Jeannine's RevealeR battled against the hungry shadows that stretched ever closer, straining to consume us.

Chapter Twenty-four – Growing Pains

The swirls of darkness closed in. They fought to swallow us, but the dazzling stream that flowed from Jeannine's RevealeR drove back the murky cloud like a fire hose beating back flame. Bubbles of soft, amber light floated everywhere, and the surface of whatever they touched rippled like a pond, and began glowing warmly. The walls encircling us shimmered, and started turning back into a nursery once more.

"You're doing it, Jeannine!" I cheered. "You're..." But she waved me off.

"Hush!" she commanded. "I'm focusing on making a picture in my mind. I've got to concentrate!"

Meanwhile, Timmy was still yanking hard on the arm of the doll-sized version of his dad, when suddenly it evaporated, and he went flying into a stack of books. The stack collapsed on top of him, burying him in old almanacs and atlases.

"Help!" he cried. "They're all over me!"

"Take it easy," I instructed as I let go of Jeannine's RevealeR and hurried over to dig him out. "You're covered in books, not monsters."

"There's a difference?" he asked as I put my flashlight in my pocket and helped him get up.

Right then I realized why Timmy gets such lousy grades.

"No wonder you need a math tutor..." I said scornfully, but then I saw his face, which was staring at a spot directly behind me and had frozen in shock.

"Uh, oh," I mumbled. I whipped my RevealeR back out of my pocket and spun around, but then I froze in shock too.

Standing on the floor beside the crib, bathed in the hazy, amber glow from Jeannine's RevealeR, was *another* Timmy. I did a double take, turning from the figure beside the crib to Timmy, who was still frozen beside me, and then back again. They were exactly the same, but for the fact that the Timmy by the crib didn't have drool all over himself and smelled a lot better.

"What *is* that?" Timmy finally stuttered. I was still gaping at the duplicate Timmy, but then turned back to Jeannine. She was standing exactly as I had left her, eyes closed and perfectly still, with a look of deep concentration on her face. The bright beam of the RevealeR in her hand was fixed directly on the figure standing by the crib.

"This must be *it*," I replied as my eyes followed the beam of light back to the figure of Timmy. "This must be the image she made in her mind! We're really seeing it!"

"This is Jeannine's image...of *me*?" Just as Timmy spoke, his monster-twin moved in closer to the crib. He

184

leaned over the railing and then waved his fingers, puffed out his cheeks, and began making funny faces.

"Ah Booga Booga Boo!" the monster-Timmy said playfully. The real Timmy watched this and grimaced.

"But...but I look ridiculous!" Timmy protested.

"About time you noticed," I snickered.

Suddenly, the sound of a baby's laughter echoed around us. The projected figure of Timmy chortled.

"Ah Booga Booga Boo!" he said again, and laughter erupted once more. I smiled, but when I looked at the real Timmy, his face was covered with the same look of horror and humiliation that mine had the day my mom visited our school and gave me a big, red-lipsticked kiss on the cheek in front of my entire gym class.

"Jeannine!" I cried out. "This one's not helping! Try thinking of something else!"

"Okay," she called back. "How about this...?" Jeannine scrunched her eyes as she focused on a new idea, and the light from her RevealeR blazed brighter. For a second I shielded my eyes with my hand, but then the light faded, and I gazed around. At first glance, the room hadn't changed, but when I looked down, I saw that toys now littered the floor.

"Wooooaah," I whispered. "Well, if Timmy doesn't wig out about this, I'll bet his mom will." Then I turned back to the crib, but it was gone. Instead, there was the other Timmy again, this time sitting reading a storybook to a small child in a striped shirt and blue overalls that sat beside him.

"...And they all lived happily ever after," he read. As he turned the page, the child smiled up at him and grasped his arm affectionately. I looked over at the real Timmy and saw his lip quiver.

"That...that's really nice," he stuttered. "But still, that little creature is so...disgusting."

"What?" I sputtered. "How can you possibly call that cute little...?" But then I stopped myself, because I remembered how I had seen the ring as just a tiny piece of gold, but Timmy saw a terrifying monster.

Timmy's not seeing this the way I do, I realized. *We are still looking at things differently.*

"Well?" Jeannine called out.

"Nice try, Jeannine," I told her. "But Timmy still isn't convinced. The baby still looks like a monster to him. What else have you got?"

Jeannine opened her eyes and glared at me. Even without her eyes closed, the images she created remained.

"Why don't *you* think of something?" she growled.

"I can't," I said. "I already tried!"

"Oh, come on, Will!" Jeannine urged. "Is it really so hard to imagine something nice about having a little brother?"

"A...little *brother*...?" I stuttered. Somehow, I hadn't thought of it that way. But once I did, a whole host of new images flooded into my brain. I closed my eyes and focused on one of them, and felt the RevealeR grow warm and bright in my hand. Then I opened them again, and squinted a bit until the scene in front of me became clear.

There was the phantom Timmy, sitting on the floor face to face with a little boy. They were both wearing baseball caps and jerseys, and each was holding a stack

of baseball cards. They took turns flipping their cards, and then the little boy cried out, "Yay! I win!" And then he picked up the cards.

"Is this for keepsies?" the boy asked. "Can I put these on my pile?"

"Why don't we make a *new* pile," the phantom Timmy answered. "A pile for both of us. Then we can share them all."

"Okay," the child said, then he held up one of the cards he had won and looked it over.

"Who's this one?" he asked.

"That's Barry Bonds," the phantom Timmy said. "Lots of people don't like him, but I think he's the best ever."

"No, *you're* the best ever," the little boy said sweetly. The phantom Timmy smiled. I looked back at the real Timmy, and he was smiling too. As his smile grew broad and warm, the darkness in the room fell back, and the fear drained from his face. For the very first time, Timmy looked at the image of what might lay ahead with no horror, disgust, or anger in his eyes, and I was certain that he must finally be seeing the little monster the same as I did. Somehow, I knew that meant Timmy's moment of truth had come.

"Timmy," I said to him. "It's time. You know what you have to do, don't you?"

He looked back at me and nodded.

"Yes," he said.

I led him over to the two figures that sat on the floor bathed in the glow of the RevealeRs. The phantom-child looked up at Timmy.

"Who are you?" the little boy asked.

Timmy reached down and put his hand gently on the boy's shoulder.

"I'm Timmy," he answered. "I...I'm your brother."

The child reached up its arms to Timmy. Timmy hesitated a moment.

"Go on," I whispered. Timmy smiled weakly, and then reached out and wrapped his arms around the child. The moment they embraced, the entire monster-nursery erupted with light, as bright and warm as the sun. The nursery walls floated back up over our heads and began to collapse into the center of the room. The furniture and toys glowed brightly, and quickly shrank. As they did, some invisible, magnet-like force set them sliding toward the glowing figures of Timmy and his little brother. Then the phantom images of Timmy and his brother shrank too. In mere moments, the whole nursery was no larger than a doll's house.

"Look!" Jeannine said. "Up there."

Directly above our heads, the walls had melted back into the shape of a golden ring. The ring shrank back to its original size, but continued to pulse with energy. All of a sudden, bursts of fire once again began shooting out from the center of its glowing form.

"Timmy, duck!" Jeannine cried as a flare flew past his head. But Timmy stood straight and tall.

"No," he said firmly. "No more. No more hiding."

And just as he spoke, the flares sputtered and the glow surrounding the ring weakened. The ring shot out another blazing spear in Timmy's direction, but he didn't duck, or even flinch.

"Timmy!" Jeannine cried.

But the flame sputtered out and died before it even reached him. Then, after one last fluttering spurt, the glimmer surrounding the ring died, and the smoldering band fell from the air into Timmy's waiting hand.

"Good work, Timmy!" I said, patting him on the back. Meanwhile, the rest of the nursery kept shrinking until it was roughly the size of a paperweight. The air froze solid around the tiny scene, making it look like a snow globe, minus all the snow. Inside the frosty sphere, the image of the nursery, with Timmy and his little brother sitting together, remained.

Timmy picked it up, and smiled at it. Then he turned to Jeannine and me.

"Thanks," he simply said.

And with that, the rest of the darkness flew from the room, replaced by the hazy glare of moonlight.

Chapter Twenty-five – Rewards

.

Timmy walked over and placed his new paperweight on his desk. Then he turned to us and opened his hand to reveal a simple golden band.

"It's your dad's wedding ring, isn't it?" Jeannine asked.

"Yes," Timmy said. "I found it in the drawer of his nightstand when I was looking for his new phone number."

I stepped up and looked over the ring with my MonsterScope. The glow, the pulsing energy, the flares; they were all gone. It was just a ring.

"It's clean," I announced. "There's nothing monstrous about it at all anymore."

"Oh, I wouldn't say *that*," Jeannine stated as she too glanced over the ring. "I think your MonsterScope may have missed something."

For a moment I froze, but then quickly scanned the ring again, searching for any sign of life.

"What is it?" I asked. "What do you see?"

"Can't you see it?" she answered. "That horrible paisley pattern engraved into the gold? It's hideous!"

I exhaled deeply and frowned. Bigelow was definitely right when he said that things are less scary when you face them with a friend, but he forgot to mention that certain friends can really get on your nerves sometimes.

"All right, enough of that," I declared. "You've got some explaining to do."

"You mean about how I knew what the monster was?" Jeannine asked.

"No, about those Powerpuff Girls panties you wear."

Jeannine's eyes bugged out worse than the time I told her that she'd accidentally tucked her skirt into her tights, and then she got very stern.

"If you ever mention that to *anyone*..."

"Don't worry," I assured her. "You're secret's safe with us." I turned to Timmy and added, "*Everyone's* secrets are safe. I think Monster Detectives should be sworn to secrecy. We'll be like doctors, except we won't stick you with needles or make you pee in a cup."

Timmy smiled, but Jeannine still looked a bit cross. I can't blame her: if I was caught wearing my Superman undershorts, I'd be pissy too. Not that I'm admitting that I *have* Superman undershorts, mind you.

"Well, I expect you'll both be treating me with more respect from now on," she said firmly.

"Jeannine, I don't know what you're talking about," I protested. "I've *always* treated you with respect."

"You treat me," she said pointedly, "like a *girl*."

"Well, if it's what you really want, from now on I'll treat you just like a boy."

"Hey, what about me?" Timmy complained. I looked back at him.

"Okay, I'll treat you just like a boy, too."

Jeannine smirked.

"Never mind," she said. "The world has too many boys as it is."

And with that, she turned and left the room. Timmy scowled at the door like he was shocked that she just up and left like that, but that's Jeannine for you.

"Now what did she mean by that?" Timmy whined. I shrugged, and shook my head.

"Girls," I said. "Who can figure them?"

Timmy's scowl broke, and he chuckled a bit.

"Yeah, you're right," he commented. "You know, my dad always says it doesn't even pay to try."

"That reminds me..." I started to say.

"...That you wanted to know more about the phone calls I made to my dad?" Timmy guessed.

"No," I said. "It reminded me that I haven't been *paid*."

"Oh," Timmy said sheepishly. "Well, your business card says, 'fee negotiable.' So what do you want?"

"I want a great big motorcycle with rocket boosters and lots of flashing lights," I answered.

I settled for the leftover chocolate bars.

The murky fog was slowly fading from the air by the time Jeannine and I left Timmy's house.

"Do come back again!" Timmy's mother called out in a sing-song voice as we trotted down the walkway.

"Wow! What got into *her*?" I said as we stepped through the gate.

But Jeannine didn't answer. In fact, she stayed silent for three whole blocks as I walked her home. I didn't know what to do, because that had never happened before, so I looked around aimlessly, and then glanced up at the night sky. It stretched black and endless in every direction, dotted here and there with only a few tiny points of light that struggled to reach us through the weakening fog. For some reason, I felt a sudden chill. I guess the quiet was making me nervous, so I pulled one of the chocolate bars out of my pocket and began eating. Now, Jeannine loves chocolate more than breathing, so when she didn't react to that, I knew something was really wrong. I took out my MonsterScope and checked her out, just to be sure that I was returning to Jeannine's mother her real daughter, and not some monster imitation. It *was* her of course, but then I looked at the spyglass itself, feeling bad that she didn't have one.

"So, I guess you're going to be a full-fledged detective after all," I told her. She blushed.

"Oh, I don't know," she said. "Maybe it'll be best if I just do the paperwork and stuff."

"What?" I said. "Why?"

Jeannine's eyes got a little teary.

"You're probably better off without me. I'm not a very good partner."

"What are you talking about? You're a *great*..."

"I left you, Will!" she suddenly cried. "I left you there to face the monsters alone!"

"But you came back," I answered. "And it was *you* that revealed the truth for all of us to see. I could never have done that without you."

"But I wasn't brave enough! You could have been eaten alive because of me!"

"Well actually, Bigelow told me that monsters don't really eat people..." I began, but as I did, Jeannine's face fell into her hands. Somehow, I could feel the guilt that was tormenting her, as real and alive as any monster, and I knew exactly what she needed to hear.

"You know," I said gently, "the first time Bigelow told me to face my monsters, I tried to run away."

Jeannine's face burst from her hands and she gasped like I had just told her that I'd caught her mother, the strict vegetarian, eating pig's feet.

"You...you did?' she sputtered.

"I did. I think maybe that's something every monster detective has to go through. I mean, no one is born knowing how to face a monster, right? We all have to learn to do it. And you did that tonight."

Jeannine's scratched her head, and then her face changed into an *I'm thinking it over* expression.

"I did, didn't I?" she finally said.

"You did," I agreed.

Jeannine's face twitched for a moment, then she finally nodded in agreement. But she still looked a little sad.

"But what about the next time?" she asked. "I mean, how do we know I'm really cut out for this?"

"You're smart and brave, and you know what to do. Bigelow said that that's all you need."

"Yes, but Bigelow *told* you that you should be a monster detective, Will. How can we ever know for sure about *me*?"

"I don't know. Maybe..." But I stopped speaking, because at that very moment a sudden burning sensation began pressing against the side of my hip.

"Owww!" I growled. "What's going on?" And I reached into my scorching hot pants pocket and pulled out a small rectangular piece of paper. Instantly, the heat disappeared. I lifted the paper to my eyes and looked at it.

"What is that?" Jeannine asked.

"My Monster Detective business card," I answered.

"You mean the card that magically appeared to you and Timmy?"

I nodded.

"What is it doing here?" she asked.

196

I smiled broadly as I handed it to Jeannine.

"Take a look," I instructed. Jeannine put on her glasses and held the card to her eyes. It read:

"If the *card* says you're a detective," I said slyly, "who are we to argue?"

Jeannine's face broke into a huge, bright smile.

"Well then," she said, straightening herself and resuming her normal, haughty tone of voice. "Does this mean I get a raise?"

"Sure," I answered, and broke her off an extra large piece of the chocolate bar. "Here you go." She took it and began eating.

"But you still don't get the big flashlight," I told her.

Jeannine went to stomp my foot, but then stopped and gave me a gentle nudge instead.

"It's okay," she giggled. "I told you: red really isn't my color." And then she blushed again, and proved it was true.

"So, Jeannine Fitsimmons," I called out in my TV announcer voice, "you've just helped solve our first case and been promoted to detective. What will you do now? Go to Disneyland?"

She giggled some more, but then straightened herself and cleared her throat.

"Actually," she said, "I think I'll use my new rank to take charge of any cases we get for the next week or so."

"Oh, you think so?" I said with a smirk. "And what makes you think I'm going to agree to that?"

"Oh, I don't think you have much of a choice," she said casually. "Seeing as how it's 8:30, and you're about to be grounded."

I looked at my watch. It read 8:32, which meant I was doomed. I handed her the MonsterScope.

"I guess I won't be needing this for a while," I said. Jeannine giggled gleefully as she took it into her hands.

"Oooh!" she cooed as she looked it over. "I can't wait to show this to my mom! Just wait until she sees what it can do! She'll freak out!"

"Um, I don't think so, Jeannine," I said. "Except for when monsters are around, the MonsterScope looks like a plain old spyglass. I'm pretty sure that's all your mom will see."

Jeannine's smile melted. She thought it over for a moment, then pulled out her RevealeR.

"Well, what about this?" she said. "Can I use it to make her see...you know, *scary* stuff?"

"It doesn't have any effect on real moms and dads," I told her. "I already tried."

"Well, what about the monsters? Seeing *those* should scare the living daylights out of her, shouldn't it?"

"She won't see them," I said sadly. "I told you: Bigelow said people can't really see what they don't understand.   And grownups never understand our monsters because…well, because they're grownups."

Jeannine frowned.

"Well then," she sighed, "I guess they'll never believe that we're really doing anything at all."

"True," I agreed. "But then I suppose that's one of the hazards of running a monster detective agency."

Jeannine slowly nodded her head, but then looked up at me and grinned.

"Well," she said, "at least this chocolate is really good."

And we walked close together in the darkness the rest of the way home.

TOP SECRET :

CONFIDENTIAL

Tips and Tricks
for
FIGHTING MONSTERS!

FOR AGENCY RECRUITS
ONLY

To all prospective Monster Detective Agency recruits:

Welcome, and thanks for thinking of joining us. Jeannine and ~~me~~ I can really use the help!

Now, I'm still no expert at this stuff, but one thing I know for sure is that you should always speak to a parent or guardian before beginning any monster detective adventure:
After all, it's their job to keep you safe from anything truly dangerous*!*

But if you're ready to begin facing your monsters, I've put in this folder some of the things I've learned about dealing with them, plus some tips given to me by my Monster Detective friend, Bigelow Hawkins. I hope they help!

But if you can't get rid of monsters on your own, don't worry or get upset. Just remember to get help from the people around you. A friend, parent, or other trusted adult can be of much more help than you may think!

And don't forget - monsters are only as big as we make them, so be brave and stay strong!

Wishing you peace, confidence, and good luck,

Will Allen - Monster Detective Third Class

Will's Tips For Fighting Monsters

1) Face your monsters

Even though it may not seem like it right away, a monster starts to shrink as soon as you confront it. I know sometimes it hurts to look, but when you face your monster, you take the first step toward conquering it.

Of course, we should always keep a safe distance away from anything that is truly dangerous.

2) Have backup

Like Bigelow says, we are always braver when we face our monsters with a friend. Find people who will support and encourage you. Friends. Family. Even Teachers, or other trusted adults. You might be surprised at how much help is out there for you.

3) Calm yourself

Exercising, listening to music, or practicing deep breathing (like my mom did the day I accidentally spilled paint all over her new carpet) are just some of the ways that you can help your body overcome the grip of fear. Monsters feed off of fear, so if we can control our fears, they won't have as much power over you.

4) Build confidence

It may seem silly, but sometimes you have to talk to yourself. Remind yourself that you can be brave and strong. Say positive things to yourself over and over. Always remember that no matter how small you feel, you are bigger on the INSIDE than any monster could ever be.

A note from Bigelow about Monsters' Thinking Traps –

Welcome, Recruits!

By now you know that Monsters feed off of your fears and other bad feelings. That is why they try to scare you or make you anxious. And they have a lot of tricks up their sleeves to get you to feel that way (not that they actually have sleeves, but you know what I mean).

Here is a list of some of the ways that monsters try to trap you into thinking dreadful thoughts.

* TRAP 1: Monster Glasses

If a monster offers you glasses, do not accept.

Monster glasses do NOT help you see better: they only let you see the bad things that happen. Monster Glasses focus on things that went wrong or were not good enough.

Seeing and remembering only bad things will worry you and can make you think that you always fail.

NEVER BELIEVE THAT!
It is *NOT TRUE* –

It is just the monsters trying to upset you.

* TRAP 2: Monster Balloons

Normal balloons are filled with air, but Monster Balloons blow up Negative things so that they look bigger than they really are.

Inflating bad things makes them become more scary and can make you feel frightened. That is like a buffet for the monsters!

* TRAP 3: Monster Trash Bins

Monster trash bins are very different from the kind *YOU* use. You put garbage, dirt, and useless things in the trash, but Monsters trash only GOOD things. Anything nice that happens is rubbished so positive things are ignored or belittled.

Rubbishing anything positive as unimportant or lucky means that you never accept that you can do good, nor believe that your successes are due to the efforts you make .

Do not fall into this trap!

You can accomplish great things if you believe in yourself!

* TRAP 4: Monster Fortune Cookies

If a monster tells your fortune, chances are it is an unpleasant one. Monsters want us expect things to go wrong. When monsters pretend to be fortune tellers, they try to make us think they know what is going to happen, and that it will be something terrible. They even whisper in our ears that the worst thing we could imagine will happen.

Expecting things to go wrong will make you feel anxious. Can you say, "Monster Dinnertime?"

Well, that will do to get you started. Now, if you you feel brave enough, then YOU can be a Monster Detective too! Join us for ...

the Monster Hunt
LIBRARY SKILLS-BUILDING ADVENTURE

Help us track down and capture any monsters that may be lurking in your local school or library, and earn your own monster detective badge!

Ask a librarian about arranging a hunt, or get info at http://j81502.wix.com/monster-hunt-program

Chronicles of the Monster Detective Agency

continues in

Will Allen

and the

HIDEOUS SHROUD

A Sneak Peak of this next episode begins HERE ->

Chapter One - Terms

First of all, let's get one thing straight – the name is Will. Will Allen. It's not Bill, Billy, William, or 'the Willster'. It's not 'Little Jimmy Neutron', like some kids at school call me, or 'Say Hey Willie' like my dad shouts out every time I come up to bat in little league. It is *definitely* not Doofus Dorkenstein, like some of the brainless jocks call me, and it is absolutely, positively not...

"Hilmar?" the substitute homeroom teacher called out. "Hilmar Allen?"

"Will," my best friend, Jeannine Fitsimmons, said after elbowing me in the ribs. "I think she means *you*."

"What?" I mumbled.

"She's taking the attendance. I think she just called out your name."

"No..." I gasped. "She didn't call out..."

"Hilmar Allen!" the teacher shouted over the chatter filling the classroom. "Present or absent?"

I put my hands over my mouth and gasped. My eyes widened in shock as I realized that one of my worst nightmares had just come true. For a moment, I thought about just letting the teacher mark me absent. Anything would be better than admitting the truth about...that *name*.

"My name is Will," I finally grumbled.

"What? What was that?"

"It's Will," I growled louder. "*Will* Allen. I'm present."

"But where's Hilmar?"

Now just so you know, I have a lot of respect for teachers. In fact, not counting Mrs. McCallister from Math class, some of my favorite people are teachers.

But obviously, this lady wasn't the sharpest tool in the shed, if you know what I mean. The qualifications for being a substitute teacher in my school must be pretty low.

"There is no Hilmar!" I shouted. "There's just me. Will. Will Allen."

"I'm sorry, but the attendance sheet says Hilmar."

Snickering began hammering my ears. I looked around the room and saw kids pointing at me and giggling. Even the stupid cartoon alphabet figures hung along the top of the blackboard seemed to be laughing. My eyes began to burn, either from the glare of the stark florescent light bouncing off the walls, or from the realization that ten years of carefully guarding my secret had just gone right down the tubes.

"Fine," I conceded, dropping my head into my hands. "Just mark me present."

But as I sat there pounding my temples, a strong odor, kind of like a cross between spoiled cheese and old socks, suddenly stung my nose. It quickly grew stronger, signaling that something foul was approaching.

210

"Hilmar?" sneered a familiar, oily voice just as I felt a hard slap on my back. "Really? *Hilmar*? Nice freakin' name, Dorkenstein."

I turned and looked up, and found a mess of stringy black hair and a large hooked nose lording high over my head. Now, I'm kind of used to looking up at people's heads, seeing as how I'm one of the shortest kids in school, but this shaggy lump made my hair stand on end. It was propped upon shoulders covered by an Ashford Middle School football team jacket with a navy front, maroon sleeves, and a bold letter 'A' on the chest, but you wouldn't think he was an athlete from the look of him – he was as sloppy as an unmade bed and his movements were awkward and twitchy. But if you saw the nasty glint in his eye, you'd never have any doubt that he was a bully.

And if you *did* have doubts about that, trust me; I know it from personal experience.

"Get lost, Jacko," I barked. "You're the last person who should make fun of someone's name." And then I turned back around.

Several kids around us gaped or howled, "OOooouuuw!" Jacko spluttered and blinked a few times, but then came around and got right in my face.

"What?" he growled. "You're mouthing off at me, Dorkenstein? *You*? You can't talk to me like that!"

He pounded his hands down on my desk and leaned toward me, but I stared right into his mousy little eyes and replied, "Obviously, genius, I *can*. I just did."

Jacko staggered as if I had hit him with a brick (Oh, if only...). He recovered himself, and grabbed my shirt and tried to pull me close, but I was braced against the desk, and didn't budge. Jacko shook his head in confusion, then his mouth started opening and closing like a fish, and his squinty eyes flickered like an old light bulb. A very dim light bulb.

"You - I'll...I'll bust your freakin'..." he began to say.

Jeannine leaned toward us and shouted, "Hey, let him go!" But before she could even get up...

"Is there a problem?" called out the substitute teacher.

Jacko blinked, but I kept staring right at him. He let go of my shirt and mumbled, "Um, no...no problem." But before he went back to his seat, he whispered, "Just you wait, runt," into my ear.

I turned and glared at him as he shuffled away like an old man, hunched over as if his head was too heavy to hold up. My bet is that's because it's filled with lead instead of brains. But even though he was probably too dense to hold a thought for very long, he was definitely nasty enough to hold a grudge for just about forever, so there wasn't much doubt that he would try to get back at me.

But I wasn't scared of him anymore. In fact, the only thing that frightened me was that word would get around about my true name. The thought of people calling me Hilmar the rest of my life is scarier than facing the most horrifying monster.

And *I* should know.

I bit my lip and groaned in frustration. For years, I had made a point of getting to every teacher before they read my name out loud and letting them know that they should call me Will. But I was so distracted that morning that I hadn't even noticed that there was a sub until it was too late. You see, my friend Jeannine had just begun telling me a wild story about how she single-handedly fought a raging battle against horrible, blood-curdling monsters. Of course, I couldn't believe it – I mean, why hadn't she called me in for backup?

You see, Jeannine and I are monster detectives. Now I know that sounds like some Xbox game or crazy fantasy to you, but it's not. Monsters are real. Real enough to bite your head off and use it as a bowling ball if you don't conquer them before they grow too strong. Jeannine and I work together as partners in our own Monster Detective Agency, but thanks to my mom and Gerald Hoffsteadler, Jeannine had to face this latest horror alone.

Wait, I'm not making sense, am I? Sorry. Jumping ahead when I tell stories is a bad habit of mine, you know, kind of like nose picking.

No, I didn't mean that *I'm* a nose picker. I was just making a point about...oh, never mind. The point is – this stuff is kind of hard for me to explain.

Let me put it another way – try picturing this: dangerous villains are running wild through the streets, looting and pillaging, causing fear and panic. Somewhere, a brave superhero quickly changes into his costume to get ready to go save the city. But just as he is about to run off to battle the evildoers, his mom waves her finger and says, "Uh, uh - You can't go...you're grounded, remember?"

Sounds crazy, right? Well, welcome to my world.

Okay, to explain all this properly, I need to go back a bit. It all started the night that Jeannine and I solved the case of the Ring of Terror (Jeannine named it that – I just call it the case where Timmy Newsome squealed like a little girl). Now, fighting monsters isn't like a football game – it doesn't end when time runs out, so I was a little late getting back home from Timmy's house. Forty-five minutes past my curfew, to be exact. And my mom was sitting in the kitchen waiting for me when I walked into the house.

"Sit," she called out the moment I came through the door. The air was thick with the scent of disinfectant and bleach as I stepped into the kitchen and saw her slumped in her chair with a spray bottle and a filthy dust rag in her hands. Her dirty-blonde curls hung loosely around her face from a very tired-looking bandana.

"Wow. Everything looks so clean," I said. My mom didn't answer. Now, my mother only does night-time house cleaning when she's really tense or upset, which meant that it was a good time for the neighbors to put on their sound-dampening headphones, because I was about to get an earful. The flowery plastic slipcover on the kitchen chair squealed as I tried to sit down quietly and sink as deep as I could into the huge trench coat and bowler hat I was wearing – the monster detective uniform I'd put together from old clothes I'd found in the attic. When my mom finally looked up, she glared at me the same as the monster in Timmy's bedroom had done, except that the monster's eyes were a little softer.

"Do you know what time it is?" she hissed.

I just nodded, and looked around. "Where's Dad?"

"Never you mind, mister!" my mom shouted, slamming her hands to the table, making an imprint in the freshly waxed surface. "Do you have any idea how worried I've been?"

"You were worried? Why? You don't believe that the monsters I fight are real, so what could you have been worried about?"

"Oh, don't throw that rubbish of yours at me!" she shrieked, popping up from the table and rising above me. "You could have been anywhere! You could have been lying in a gutter for all I knew!"

I shrank back from her blistering screams. Let me tell you - if I ever want my head bitten off, there is never a need for me to wait around for monsters to do it.

"I...I told you I was going to Timmy Newsome's house. You could have just called them..."

Thankfully, that bit of logic acted like a splash of cold water in my mom's face. She instantly quieted, except for the sound of her teeth grinding. Her eyes closed, and she inhaled a long, loud breath. As the air whistled into her lungs, she waved her arms in a circle and brought her hands together as though she was praying (which is exactly what I felt like doing), then backed away and sat back down in her seat at the table.

"You're grounded," she said flatly as her eyes slowly reopened.

"But...but don't you even want to know why I'm late?" I asked.

"Does it have anything to do with that ridiculous monster hunting thing you say you're doing?"

"Actually, *yes*," I said proudly. "Jeannine and me, we just solved our first case together! See, Timmy Newsome was being haunted by this terrible harpy that was..."

"Then *no*, I don't want to know why you're late," she said. "Grounded. Two days. School. Home. Your room. That's it. And no phone, video games, or TV."

"Two days?" I gasped. "But...but doesn't it count for something that I saved someone from horrifying monsters? That I faced terrible danger and came home safe and sound?"

My mother studied me thoughtfully.

"Yes, that does count for something," she muttered, tapping her index finger to a spot on her chin that was already worn and red as she stared into space. She tapped some more, and then looked back down at me.

"Make it *three* days," she said. "Now go get yourself cleaned up! You look like you've been playing in a land fill. And don't you dare throw those filthy clothes on the floor. I just mopped it." And she then stormed off, muttering under her breath, "They never taught us about things like this in child psychology class..."

I just sat there, feeling as frustrated as the day I got punished for throwing up all over my mom's new carpet (Hey, *she* was the one who insisted that I eat those asparagus dumplings she made). But I guess I couldn't really expect any better: after all, I *was* out past my curfew. And seeing as how grown-ups can't even *see* kids' monsters, I honestly couldn't expect my mom to believe that the reason I got home late was because I was too busy helping Timmy Newsome fend off a gruesome harpy while dodging spears of flame that came from his father's wedding ring.

Even though it was the truth. But then as any kid knows, grownups have no use for a truth they don't want to hear.

"This is just so unfair," I muttered as I stood and strode into the living room on the way to the stairs.

"What was that?" a voice called out from deep within the cushions of the easy chair by the far wall. My eyes followed the voice across the room, over the pristine leather couch that is so beautiful that no one is allowed to sit on it, and past the exotic coffee table shaped like a series of interlocking snakes. Behind the table, above a stack of neatly laid out art books that are the only items in the whole house with dust on them, sat a rickety old lounger that clashed with all of the other furniture in the room. Spread open wide in front of the chair was an upright newspaper that blocked from view all but the hands of the person who sat holding it.

"I said it's not fair, Dad!" I barked at the back of the sports section. The newspaper didn't flinch, but the chair's vinyl cushions groaned as my father leaned forward to speak.

"Well, Will," my dad's voice began, "It's about time you learned that…"

"Life's not fair, so I better get used to it," I recited. "Is that what you were going to tell me?"

The newspaper ruffled, and then dropped several inches, revealing thinning grey hair, a broad, ruddy forehead, and finally, my dad's puzzled eyes.

"How did you know I was going to say that?" he asked. I just rolled my eyes.

"The same way I knew where to find your missing golf club or what that rattling sound was in the back of the car. I'm a detective, Dad!"

My father chuckled, "No, really…" I frowned at him.

"All right, Dad," I replied. "The real reason I knew you'd say that is because it's what you *always* say. It's the same thing you told me after I got picked on by that bully."

My father's eyes squinted for a second, but then he lifted the paper back up.

"Well, that's because it's true," he said, and then the cushions made a splooshy sound as he settled back into them. He didn't speak again, and I didn't feel like talking to the back of the newspaper, so I continued to the stairs and up to my room.

Chapter Two - Turnabout

When I got to my room, I stumbled in, tossed my ratty bowler hat over to my desk, and plopped down, face first, onto my bed without so much as taking off my shoes and coat.

Hey, you'd be tired too if you'd just been struggling with horrifying, insufferable creatures.

And that's after fighting monsters all night.

But even though I was exhausted, I couldn't help tossing and turning in my bed.

"Grounded!" I grumbled as I sat up, arms crossed. Around me the walls of my room, which are normally sickeningly cheery-looking, brooded darkly in the moonlight. "Grounded for doing good! Punished for being a hero! It's so unfair!"

Still, the more I sat there moping, the more I knew that there was nothing I could do to change my parents' minds, and no point in whining about it either. I squirmed weakly a bit, but then resolved, as I lay back down and my eyes began to flutter closed, that I would simply take my punishment quietly.

When I come home tomorrow, I'll just go right to my room, I thought as my mind grew fuzzy. *At least then I'll be able to catch up on my schoolwork.* And I would have done just that, but for the card.

That would be my special, Monster Detective Agency business card. It's the card that magically appears to kids who have a monster, telling them to come to me, Will Allen, monster detective third class, to get help. Only somehow the card got all mixed up, because the next time it appeared, it sent Gerald Hoffsteadler to...

Hold on. I'm jumping ahead again. Just wait – we'll get to that part in a minute.

So anyway, the next morning started out pretty much like most every other day: with the shrill whine of my alarm clock making me stuff my head under the pillow. My hand banged its way blindly across the end table until it either hit the snooze button or smashed the buzzer, I'm not sure which. My eyes were still half shut as I rolled out of bed and threw off my Chicago Cubs bedspread, which had somehow wrapped itself around me as I slept, then staggered over to the window and opened the shades to let the sun wake up the bright blue walls of my room. I made my bed (sort of), and then tottered down the hall to the bathroom to wash up. I splashed my face, but when I looked up from the sink I gasped in horror at my reflection.

"Oh no!" I whispered to myself as the mirror revealed that I was still wearing my slimy monster detective clothes from the night before. "I'm *doomed*! If mom finds out she'll... "

"Will, are you awake?" My mother's voice rang out at that very moment.

"No!" I shouted back, but then quickly slapped my mouth closed.

Yes, I know that's like locking the barn door after the horse has escaped, but I couldn't help myself. I peeked out the door to make sure no one was in the hallway, then quickly scooted back to my room. With the fog washed from my eyes, the morning light spreading through my room showed that monster slime, which had splattered on my jacket during the previous night's adventure, had dripped all over my bed and floor. I grabbed a dirty towel from my hamper and wiped up the trail of goo, then cleaned off my hair, face, and hands too, just in case. After all, you don't think I would go to school looking like a slob, do you?

Wait. Don't answer that.

Next, I changed my clothes, putting on chinos and a rugby shirt, and then combed my hair and brushed my teeth as usual. But after that there was still one more chore to perform. I cautiously drew on over to a large glass fishbowl on my shelf which was half-filled with dirt, grass, and leaves. It shook a little as I approached, and as I drew closer, something under the leaves rustled. I leaned in for a better look, when suddenly a set of vicious fangs sprang from the underbrush and snapped hard at my face...

- -

This concludes our preview of **Will Allen** and the **HIDEOUS SHROUD**

To continue this adventure, or to read any of the other volumes in the

Chronicles of the Monster Detective Agency

find copies of our books at Barnes & Noble, Amazon, or wherever fine books are sold!

Common Core Literacy Standards-based Review Questions

Below is a series of review questions matched to
Common Core Literacy Standards CCSS.ELA-LITERACY.RL.2-5.1-10

Key Ideas and Details:

A}- Demonstrate understanding of key details in a text.

1)   What was Will Allen's FINAL monster?

2)   What was revealed to be Will Allen's HIDDEN BEAST? What did Will discover was Timmy Newsome's HIDDEN BEAST? Why were they so different?

3)   What event set free Will Allen's HIDDEN BEAST?

4)   According to Bigelow Hawkins, what is the source of the RevealeR's power?

5)   Why did the monsters get larger and more powerful when Will and his friends tried to run away from them?

B}- Recount stories and determine their central message, lesson, or moral.

6)   What, according to the story, must a person do to defeat monsters? What does this imply about dealing with fears and anxieties?

7)   Why do you think light made the monsters shrink? If light lets us see the truth about things that scare us, would that make monsters more or less scary? Why?

8)   Why did Timmy's monster look different to Will than it did to Jeannine? What quality does a person need to have in order for them to truly see someone else's monster? Why?

C}- Describe how characters respond to major events and challenges. Explain how their actions contribute to the sequence of events.

9)   What was Will Allen's reaction when his HIDDEN BEAST was finally revealed? What does Will's description of the look in his father's eyes say about Will and his father?

10)   How did Will Allen react when he first uncovered Timmy Newsome's ring monster? How was his reaction different the second time he saw Timmy's monster?

11)   What similarity was there in the way the characters reacted when each of them first saw a monster? Was this reaction helpful, or did they need to develop a new way of responding?

12)   What characteristics of Jeannine Fitsimmons allowed her to see Timmy Newsome's monsters more clearly than Will, and what role did that play in helping to uncover Timmy's HIDDEN BEAST?

Craft and Structure:

A)- Determine the meaning of words and phrases as they are used in a text, distinguishing literal from nonliteral language.

13)   What was the name of Will Allen's special flashlight? What does the name suggest about the flashlight's special power?

14)   What was heralded whenever Will Allen suddenly felt cold? What might those 'chills' represent?

15)   List and explain 3 metaphors and/or similes used in the story.

16) How might Timmy Newsome describe Will's first visit to his room that is different from the way Will's described it? What explanation might he give for kicking Will out?

17) Do you think Will was completely honest in tellIng his story? What parts might YOU tell differently if you were telling this story.

18) What differences might there be in this story if it was told by Jeannine instead of Will?

Integration of Knowledge and Ideas:

A}- Use information gained from the illustrations and words to demonstrate understanding of the story's characters, setting, or plot.

19) Look at the illustration in chapter four of Will sitting in the chair. Based upon that picture, how do you think he was feeling as he waited for something to happen?

20) In the illustrations in chapter two, what similarity is there in the stance of Will's mother and that of his teacher? What do those images suggest about their attitudes toward Will? Were those attitudes justified?

21) In chapter twenty-three, there is an illustration of Timmy Newsome fighting the pull of the monster on a doll-sized figure of his father. What does this suggest is his secret fear?

B}- Compare and contrast the themes, settings, and plots of stories written about the same characters, as well those of others in the same genre.

22) How do Chronicles of the Monster Detective Agency stories differ in theme and content from *Goosebumps* books?

23) If you have gone on to read ***Will Allen and the Hideous Shroud,*** how do the monsters Will Allen faces in that story differ from those in this volume? What changes in Will and his friends might this represent?

Additional review questions and activities:

23) What does Will's confrontation with the bully reveal about him? What point do you think the author is making about bullies in general? Do you agree?

24) Describe Will's relationship with his father. After reading about Will's HIDDEN BEAST, why do you think Will reacted so angrily when his father entered his room in chapter four? How is this different from what first appeared to be the reason?

25) Monsters in this book represent things people are scared of. Might *you* have some 'monsters'? Do you think parents have 'monsters' too? What might they look like?

26) Create your own monster. Draw a picture, or make a model with clay and/or other craft materials. Use your imagination and go wild! Give it as many heads, eyes, and legs as you want! Then give it a name. Can you make up a story around your monster?

Plus: for FREE teacher's guides, character profiles, bonus adventures, and additional activities, visit out review materials webpage:
http://j81502.wix.com/monsterdetectives#!bonus-materials